ONE MURDER AT A TIME

They'd been an odd couple, brought together by a murder investigation and discovering that they had an amazing chemistry . . . Hobart Lindsey is a suburban, middle-class, conservative-minded claims adjuster and Marvia Plum is a tough city cop who has fought her way up from the street. But now the couple have split and gone their own ways, both pursuing a series of mysterious crimes. Then fate throws them together again, reuniting them at the scene of a lurid murder . . .

RICHARD A. LUPOFF

ONE MURDER AT A TIME

The Casebooks of Lindsey & Plum

Complete and Unabridged

LINFORD
Leicester

First published in Great Britain

First Linford Edition
published 2012

British Library CIP Data

Lupoff, Richard A., *1935* –
  One murder at a time. - -
  (Linford mystery library)
  1. Detective and mystery stories.
  2. Large type books.
  I. Title II. Series
  813.5′4–dc23

ISBN 978–1–4448–1366–1

Published by
F. A. Thorpe (Publishing)
Anstey, Leicestershire

Set by Words & Graphics Ltd.
Anstey, Leicestershire
Printed and bound in Great Britain by
T. J. International Ltd., Padstow, Cornwall

This book is printed on acid-free paper

1

Star Lotus

'Why me?' Marvia Plum asked.

Dorothy Yamura gave her the kind of look that cops give other cops when they're speaking in private. No civilians around. No media around. No politicians around. No civil rights activists around.

'You know, I'd like to be treated as a cop for once. I like to think I made sergeant because I'm a good cop, not because I'm an African-American female.'

'Don't forget to add single mother.' Dorothy Yamura leaned back in her chair. 'And I'd like to think I made lieutenant because I'm a good cop, too, Marvia. Not because the old Irishman was suffering from white guilt over the detention camps. Well, O'Hara's retired now and I've got his job and you've got mine and we've got a serial killer in Berkeley. At least, I think we've got a serial killer.'

Marvia grinned, not happily. 'How many bodies does it take to make the case? How many have there been now, five, six?'

'Five.'

'And you're sure they're the work of one killer?'

Dorothy Yamura shook her head. She wore civilian clothes, the dress-for-success look. With her glossy hair pulled behind her head and her thin northern Japanese features, she looked like a bank executive or the newest partner in a major California law firm. She did not look like a cop.

Neither did Marvia Plum — or she would not have, to an observer from an earlier era. But in this age, a black female in a smart, form-fitting police sergeant's uniform did not draw the stares and comments she once would have.

'We called in our tame consultant from the University,' Yamura explained. 'These murders have some of the earmarks of the classic serial killer. But others are missing. In fact, some of the signs point straight *away* from a serial killer. Some of them

2

make me wonder if they're even connected.'

She extended a slim, meticulously manicured hand and tapped a glossy fingernail on the top folder on her desk. 'Look at these, Marvia. How familiar are you with this series?'

'I've followed them. Remember, Telegraph Avenue was my old beat. I've had enough cases that centered there. It's kind of a hobby, now, following the incident reports and the stats. Everybody knows this town would be a dead duck if the Telegraph merchants had to close up and move away. But every time we try and get a handle on the crime there, you'd think we were trying to repeal the Bill of Rights.'

Now it was Dorothy Yamura's turn to grin wryly. 'That's why I want to pull all these cases together. We're going to work on the notion that they are connected. If they are, if we're right and we can figure out what's going on and catch the perp, we can get a major bad guy off the streets and stop these killings. If we're wrong . . . well, we can still tackle the cases one by one and solve them that way. Like the Twelve-Step people say, *One day at a time.*'

Marvia Plum nodded. 'One murder at a time.'

'Okay.' Yamura seemed relieved. 'What's your plan?'

Plum pulled the stack of folders toward herself. They slid smoothly on the polished glass on top of Yamura's desk. 'I have to study these, of course. And I want to talk to your pet bigdome, and to the people who are bringing the pressure.'

'Sounds good to me. Okay, jot this down. Consultant at UC is Martha Rachel Bernstein, Ph.D. Here's her phone number. And Mistress Moonflower, she runs that shop called Woodstock West on the avenue.'

'I know it well. And I know Mistress Moonflower.' Marvia Plum made a sour face.

'Yes. Moonflower's after us to solve these murders. Says that the publicity is killing trade. Half of her customers are fourteen-year-old kids from Walnut Creek who think it's daring to take the train into

4

Berkeley and buy black light posters and rolling papers and take them home with them. Now all the mommies and daddies are cracking down on their little darlings and Woodstock West is losing money.'

'Moonflower has no other ax to grind?'

Dorothy Yamura gave her little, breathy laugh. She seemed reluctant to let the laughter out except in tiny, rationed bursts. 'Woodstock West got hit by a burglar or burglars. You must have read the report. Or at least seen it on the news. Channel Two loved it. I think there was even a little network pickup.'

'Oh, yes. Jimi Hendrix's guitar. The very one he used at the Monterey Pops in the Summer of Love. I did see the footage. That was the one he poured lighter fluid all over and set fire to.'

'Yes. That was considered art in 1967. The Who smashed 'em up and Jimi set 'em on fire.' She got a faraway look. Marvia wondered where Dorothy Yamura had been in 1967 but there were some things· that a sergeant did not ask a lieutenant. Even if they were friends.

Marvia Plum stood up and hefted the

stack of folders in her arms. She started to leave Dorothy Yamura's office.

'Oh, one more thing.' Plum turned back. 'You know Councilmember Hanson?'

'Sherry Hanson? Sure. Never met a cop she didn't hate.'

'Right. Well, she's interested in this case.'

'Why doesn't that surprise me?'

'She's been burning up the phone lines. She says this is a conspiracy between the business interests and the fascist police to ethnic-cleanse Berkeley.'

'Ethnic cleansing? What does that have to do with it?'

'Her phrase, Marvia. You better call her up, or better yet go see her at City Hall. At least she can't say it's a white male conspiracy.'

'No, her favorite line is that I've sold out both my race and my sex.'

Yamura waved her hand. 'Do your best, Marvia. Just do your best.' She ran her long graceful fingers through her long, glossy hair. 'Oh, I meant to tell you. Sally O'Hara sends her love.'

Marvia grinned. Sally O'Hara was the

old lieutenant's daughter. She'd refused to join the Berkeley force. Didn't want to ride her daddy's coattails. So she'd joined the Chicago PD. She was a rising star in that city, and when her father retired he'd gone to live with her.

'What's new with Sally?'

'Just made detective. I've been keeping her posted on these killings, just for old times sake.'

Marvia Plum left Yamura's office, made her way to her own desk and started through the manila folders. So Yamura was keeping Sally O'Hara posted just for old times sake. Marvia believed that as much as she believed that the check was in the mail.

She would visit both Mistress Moonflower and Councilmember Hanson, and it might be a good idea to have a chat with Professor Bernstein, too. But first, she needed to review the case — or cases — to date.

There had been five fatalities. Marvia looked for a pattern; she knew that, if you could find something in common among a series of crime victims, you had taken your first step toward finding the criminal. She made a set of file cards, one for each subject, filling in the victim's name, race, sex, age, and other details. There was a mug-shot of each victim in the folder, some from older files, some clearly made in the county morgue; she carried the pictures to the photocopier and made copies of them, attaching one to each file card.

OTTO TIMMINS, 45, wm, USN Vietnam vet, chronic alcoholic, multiple arrests for harassing patrons of local cafés & restaurants. Body found in dumpster, shot in back of neck w/.22 cal. pistol.

LaTONIA JONES, 11, bf, homeless, elementary school dropout, professional lookout and runner for known crack dealers. Collapsed on sidewalk in front of Gene's Jeans, taken to County Hospital, died of combination drug overdose and poisoning (heroin contaminated with strychnine).

BILL SZYMANSKI, 26, wm, and ROBIN 'MAINMAN' CAMPBELL, 31, bm. Both killed by single shotgun blast while naked together in sleeping bag in

People's Park. Witnesses describe 'big, bearded guy who roared like an animal' leaving scene with shotgun. No other details due to darkness.

IMACULATA MARTINEZ, 66, lf, found in restroom of What's Flat and Round with a Hole in the Middle, multiple stab wounds. Was seen entering restroom with another woman, both dressed in multiple layers of rags. (What's Flat and Round with a Hole in the Middle is leading Telegraph Avenue record store.)

Marvia laid out the cards like a poker hand and studied them. Three males, two females. Two of the males were gay. One of the females was a drug abuser. Ages ranged from 11 to 66. Two white males, one black male, one black female, one latina female. Two shotgunned, one poisoned, one stabbed, one shot with a pistol.

All were homeless, all hung out in People's Park and/or the Telegraph Avenue area.

What in the world did that add up to?

Marvia went to the locker room and

changed from her sergeant's blues into a set of neat but casual civvies — jeans, a plaid button-up shirt, a light cloth jacket. The jacket concealed both her badge and her service revolver. She wasn't exactly going undercover — in fact, she wasn't going undercover at all — but she didn't want to flaunt her presence by poking around in uniform.

Her first stop was Woodstock West.

She stepped from the bright sunlight and midday bustle of Telegraph Avenue into a very different, very special zone. The interior of the shop was dimly lighted, with Indian-print drapes filtering out most of the sunlight. The air was almost tangible in its thickness. She could almost feel the slowly rising incense on her tongue, it was so thick.

Black light posters covered the walls. There were astronomical scenes, nudes, drawings of cannabis plants, mind-twisting M.C. Escher prints, reproductions of Fillmore Ballroom posters. An oil portrait of Jimi Hendrix dominated one wall.

Mistress Moonflower was behind the glass counter, selling rolling papers to a couple of UC freshwomen who had their arms against each other. The shorter of the two customers snuggled her head into the shoulder of the taller. The taller customer looked over her shoulder and smiled down at Marvia. Sure, sweetie-pie, Marvia thought. Black or white, straight or gay, sisterhood is strong. You bet.

Mistress Moonflower recognized Marvia and nodded.

Marvia said, 'I need to talk to you, Myrna.'

Mistress Moonflower frowned and turned toward the back of the store. 'Star Lotus, front.'

A younger, beefier version of Mistress Moonflower emerged through a wall of hanging prints. Mistress Moonflower led Marvia into a cramped office-cum-stock room. Moonflower wore a kerchief woven through her curly black hair, a filmy blouse and billowing skirt. The blouse was open to her sternum. An eye-of-god was visible, tattooed between her breasts. She was barefoot and wore an anklet with a tinkling bell.

She said, 'My name is Moonflower.'

11

Marvia bit her lower lip. 'Your business permit says Myrna Gersh.'

Mistress Moonflower shook her head. 'I left Myrna Gersh behind years ago. Threw her off a mountain in Nepal.'

'Yeah, right. They ever find the body?'

'We shared this body. That day Myrna Gersh left the plane and I was born, Mistress Moonflower.'

'Okay. What do you know about the series of murders in the Telegraph area?'

'The Tallyman.'

'What?'

'The Tallyman. He appears, he takes his tally and he disappears. That's what we call him now. The Tallyman.'

'Lieutenant Yamura says that you represent the local merchants.'

'Unofficially.'

'Are you concerned?'

'We're frightened.'

'The Tallyman going after storekeepers? Shoppers? Students?'

'You never know who's next.'

Marvia reached into a jacket pocket and laid out her victim cards. 'What do you make of these?'

The curtains parted and Star Lotus stuck her head into the back room. Mistress Moonflower hissed, 'Stay out there. Wait on customers. Make yourself useful.'

Star Lotus withdrew.

'Look, we were hit, Officer. I mean, Woodstock West was hit. I don't know if the Tallyman did it, or somebody else, but we need protection from the police, not harassment.'

'I know, Jimi Hendrix's guitar. Totally burned, beyond repair.'

'It was a holy relic. If we could only recover it . . . '

'Right. It's practically the Shroud of Turin. Look, I want you to look at these cards and photos and tell me if you knew any of these people.'

Mistress Moonflower looked at the cards and the photos. She looked up at Marvia and shrugged. 'Sure, I knew them.'

'All of them?'

'They were all Telly regulars. Panhandlers, street people. Sometimes they'd come into the store and demand money. Sometimes they'd want to use the back room. I never let them. When they pestered my customers I'd shoo them out. Call the cops if I had to. Lot of help that was, they always knew how long it would take the fuzz to arrive and split just in the nick of time.'

The fuzz, Marvia thought. Marvia Plum, Sergeant Fuzz.

'Who killed them?'

'They're all dead, aren't they?'

'Who killed them?'

'How the hell should I know? The Tallyman did it.'

'Who's the Tallyman?'

Mistress Moonflower shrugged. One breast popped halfway out of her shirt. She said, 'Oops,' and readjusted herself.

Marvia Plum started for the curtain that would bring her back into the storefront. She could hear customers talking with Star Lotus. It sounded as if Star Lotus was making a big sale. Marvia stopped and inquired, 'I'm curious, Myrna. How's business lately?'

Mistress Moonflower shrugged a little more carefully. ''Bout the same as ever.'

'Tallyman isn't scaring your customers off, then?'

''Bout the same as ever.'

Marvia crossed Telegraph and headed down the block toward People's Park. She strolled along the sidewalk, not entering the park. She turned back toward the campus and stood in front of a sorority house. In five minutes one of her park snitches showed up.

'I saw you walk past the park. I could use a little bread.'

Lawsamarcy! Use a little bread. 'What do you have for me?'

'I don't know. Ask me a question.'

'Who's the Tallyman?'

The snitch was wearing a ragged tube-top and sweat pants. Between them, her belly showed. It was smudged with ordinary dirt and a little of what seemed to be dried mustard. She wore a navel-ring from which a silver chain and crucifix dangled over the top of her pants. She said, 'Don't ask me that.'

'You followed me, Vangie.'

'I know. Ask me something else.'

'What do you know about LaTonia Jones?'

Despite the bright sunlight, Vangie shivered. 'A lot of people didn't like her. She worked for some crack dealers. They'd show up generally around dusk, you know, when we get our campfires started, and she'd play lookout for them. In case the pigs were coming. Pardon me, Sergeant.'

'Yeah. Why didn't they like her?'

'You know.' Vangie twisted her torso and flung her hair off her face. Marvia jerked away.

'I don't know. That's why I asked you.'

'You know. Uh, well, you know, there are some moms in the park. They don't want their brats getting hooked. You know, LaTonia kind of, well, recruited. Users, hookers. Sometimes guys come by the park in cars, especially at night. They like little kids, girls or boys.'

'Vangie, who killed LaTonia?'

'I dunno. The Tallyman. Can I have some bread?'

'You'll have to do better than that. You haven't given me anything I don't already know.' Marvia Plum turned away and started toward the UC campus.

16

She felt Vangie's hand on her shoulder. She wasn't surprised. 'Somebody saw LaTonia just before — before. It was just about sundown. Some big car pulled up by the park. She went over. I saw her lean in, then come out with something.'

'Come on, Vangie. Something — what?'

'I don't know. I guess it was a needle.'

'And she shot up and died. And somebody stole the needle and used it again, probably.' Almost certainly. The needle had never been found. But there were no more strychnine deaths, so whoever took it had apparently had the brains to rinse it out, at least.

'What kind of car?'

'Big. Foreign. I don't know.'

'What color was it?'

'White.'

'Japanese? German? American?'

'I don't know. One of those English cars, I think.'

'A Rolls?'

'No. I think they call it a Jagger or something.'

'Who was driving?'

'I couldn't see.'

'Try and remember something. Man or woman?'

'I don't know.' Marvia turned away. Again, the hand. 'A woman.'

'Age? Black or white?'

'No age, any age. White.'

'That's all? What next?'

'She drove away, that's all. I didn't follow her, for God's sake.'

Marvia Plum handed her a folded bill and Vangie trotted away, back toward the park.

Marvia headed for City Hall. She found Councilmember Hanson in her office.

'I came to talk about the Tallyman.'

'The who?'

'They're calling the Telly killer the Tallyman. I heard it in one of the shops and again at People's Park.'

'Wonderful. Police Department's paying some attention at last, are they? I roasted the chief enough.'

'Lieutenant Yamura assigned me the case, Councilmember Hanson.'

'You can call me Sherry, sister. We're all sisters.'

'No we aren't.'

Councilmember Hanson looked angry. 'I should have known. I checked up on your background. You were in the army. You were a cop there too. What is it you like, carrying a gun around? Wearing a uniform?'

'I'm not wearing one now.'

'What have you learned?'

'I report to Lieutenant Yamura. You can get your information from her.'

'Sergeant, you're in the Berkeley Police Department, not the Gestapo. I want to know what you've learned.'

Marvia counted to ten. 'All I've got is a list of victims and a name. The Tallyman. He could be anybody.' There was the hulking figure who walked away from Bill Szymanski and Robin Campbell's sleeping bag. She didn't know about the woman who entered the restroom with Imaculata Martinez, or the woman in the white Jagger — it must be a Jaguar — who gave the needle to LaTonia Jones. If Hanson didn't know all that, it was just as well.

'I want regular reports on this matter,' the councilmember was saying. 'These are people of color, they're poor people, they're the victims of society, and now they're being murdered.'

'Yes, ma'am.'

'They're your people, Marvia.' She smiled. 'What about that little Jones girl?'

'The crack dealer's lookout?'

'That child needed help, Marvia.'

'She got a lot of that, didn't she, Councilmember? I have an appointment.'

Marvia Plum phoned Dr. Martha Rachel Bernstein at the university, ascertained that she would be in her office for the next hour, arranged to go see her. She left her car at police headquarters and walked to the campus. There seemed to be more street vendors than ever. Business was booming. The customers didn't even look grubby today — a combination of student types, workers on their breaks, shoppers. There were even some parents with small children in tow, apparently in from the suburbs for a day in Berkeley. Marvia Plum hadn't seen much of that in years.

Martha Rachel Bernstein, Ph.D. was short and heavyset, more muscular than fleshy. Her office overlooked Bancroft Way and Telegraph Avenue. She peered up through thick bifocals when Marvia Plum stood in her doorway and said, 'Met you before, Sergeant. Remember that case with the stolen Duesenberg phaeton?'

Marvia said, 'I surely do. But I'd forgot that we worked on that one.'

'Okay. I guess white people all look the same anyhow. You want to talk about the Tallyman.'

'You know about that. I seem to be the only one who hasn't known that name all along.'

'Lieutenant Yamura sent me the information on these killings. Five victims. I'm a sociologist, you know, not a psychologist.'

'Aren't they pretty close?'

'Sometimes. Anyway — hey, why are you standing there like you might run away any second, come on in and close the door and sit down. Isn't this a palace?'

Marvia complied.

'I studied the victims' profiles. Also had

an interesting talk with my friend, Dr. Chih.'

'I don't know — '

'Chih Yuan. Good friend of mine. Looks at the relationship of sociology and economics. Effect of family constellations on crime stats and vice versa. Smart woman. Brilliant woman. Taiwanese.'

'Chinese?'

'Taiwanese. Hates Chinese. Says that Taiwan is a colony.'

Marvia shifted in her chair. 'Look, Doctor — '

'Martha.'

'I'm not really interested in whether Taiwan is a colony of China or China's a colony of Taiwan. I've got five murders here.'

'Don't sneer at Dr. Chih's work.'

'I don't mean to sneer at her work. But I'm concerned with my own work. It looks as if we've got a serial killer loose, only we're not even sure of that. Maybe I really am in the wrong department. Maybe we should get a shrink.'

'I want her to join us.' Martha Bernstein reached for the telephone.

When Marvia Plum didn't object, she punched another extension and muttered into the mouthpiece. Moments later Dr. Chih swept into Bernstein's office. Bernstein introduced her and Marvia Plum.

Dr. Chih flung herself into a vacant chair. She sprawled with her feet in front of her. She wore her hair in a crewcut; she looked as if a giant fuzzy black caterpillar had chosen her for best friend. She wore a black tee shirt with a larger-than-life-size portrait of Marilyn Monroe on the chest. She wore tight jeans and white, low-top sneakers.

She gave Marvia Plum a look. 'Rache says you're interested in these murders. The boys in the bag and those others.'

'I am.'

'Why?'

Marvia nearly let go a giggle. 'It's my job, Dr. Chih. I'm a cop. We catch murderers.'

'Why?'

Marvia shook her head. 'Don't ask me to philosophize. We have laws, we have cops to enforce the laws, we have more cops who try to catch people who break the laws. After that it's up to the DA and the judge and the whole rest of the system.'

Dr. Chih had closed her eyes during Marvia Plum's response. When Marvia finished, she opened her eyes again and said, 'You don't have any theory about morality or the social contract or repairing rents in the fabric of civilization?'

'I'm just doing my job.'

'Because the Berkeley *Voice* and the Oakland *Trib* have been carrying on about how this town is losing its collective conscience, and besides the local merchants are losing business hand over fist because people are scared to come into town.'

'I've heard that.'

Dr. Chih grinned. Her teeth were big and very white. 'You see, I'm interested in the economic effects of social change. And a funny thing's been happening. The papers are wrong. The local merchants are prospering. Every time one of these troubled souls is removed violently from our midst, there's a momentary scare, and then local business goes *up*. Do you think that's odd?'

'I noticed it myself. On my way over here.'

'Ah-hah.'

'But where do we go from there? Do you think it would be a good thing to let these murders continue?'

'I'm a social scientist, not a moralist. I observe and report, and I try to understand. I don't judge.'

Marvia swung in her chair. 'Dr. Bernstein, what's your take?'

'How?'

'Any idea who's doing the killings? Based on what you know about the victims?'

Bernstein tapped a yellow pencil on the edge of an old, smoked-glass ashtray on the corner of her desk. Marvia saw a sealed brown package in the ashtray. Philip Morris cigarettes. How long had they been there?

'It's somebody who knows the Telegraph area well. Maybe somebody who lives here, or has lived here.'

'Motive?'

'You sure you want me and not a shrink?'

'Go for it, Doctor.'

'I think it's political. Or moral. Maybe even religious.'

Dr. Chih asked a question. 'Why do people kill people, Sergeant Plum? You deal with it every day. I only read murder mysteries, and I like the old-fashioned kind where the wicked nephew poisons the wealthy uncle so he can marry the beautiful adventuress.'

Marvia nodded. 'Yes. People murder for money. There was that case in San Francisco where a couple of smart cookies were marrying rich old men with coronary problems and overdosing them with their own heart medicine. And of course those sweet brothers in LA who shotgunned mommy and daddy for their millions.'

'My point exactly.' Dr. Chih shifted her weight and crossed her ankles. 'These people had nothing. They were down-and-outers, sleeping in the park.'

'Well, we have turf wars. The crack

dealers have brought back the old Al Capone style drive-by's. And there's the hold-up artist who panics and shoots the convenience store clerk. Sometimes a handful of customers for good measure. And the disgruntled worker who takes a Tek-9 back to the office and blows away half the staff.' Marvia Plum shook her head. 'It's a sorry business.'

Dr. Bernstein tapped her ashtray for attention. Marvia guessed it was her habit. 'Don't forget domestic violence.'

Marvia said, 'I don't.' After a moment of silence she added, 'But none of these account for Otto Timmins and Imaculata Martinez and the rest of my folks.' Her file cards and photos were still spread on Dr. Bernstein's desk. She pressed them down with her fingertips, slid them around like a slick dealer.

Dr. Bernstein said, 'What if you have more than one killer?'

'Why would you think that?'

'Dr. Chih's notion of a religious vendetta.'

'That info I don't have. And that's something we've avoided, at least. We don't have Catholics and Protestants killing each other, or Muslims and Jews.'

Dr. Chih pushed herself upright in her seat. 'That is not what I meant by religious. I meant, someone who resents the lifestyle of these people.'

Marvia was surprised by that suggestion. 'Who would envy these lost souls? An alcoholic ex-sailor, an eleven-year-old crack lookout, a 66-year-old bag lady, and a pair of gay lovers reduced to sharing a sleeping bag in People's Park. Who *could* envy them?'

'No, I did not say envy.' Dr. Chih sat straighter still. Marvia Plum realized that she was quite tall, with square shoulders and a slim body. 'I said, *resent*. Resentment and envy are similar but they are not identical. I agree with you, it would be hard to find anyone who envied these homeless souls. But think of someone whose whole lifestyle and livelihood is tied to more conventional values. Someone who feels constricted by a job with regular hours, oppressed by taxes and rent bills and license fees and all the other impedimenta of modern urban life.'

'Okay,' Marvia nodded. 'And that person is maybe on her way home from a hard day's work — '

'Or maybe she's running an errand on her lunch break,' Dr. Bernstein put in.

'Or maybe . . . ' Dr. Chih stood and crossed to Martha Rachel Bernstein's single, small window. ' . . . she just looks out the window and she sees the contrast between the hardworking little worker bees like herself, and the lazy, sybaritic drones lounging in the park or panhandling on the avenue — '

'And suppose a group of such like-minded, hardworking, law-abiding, productive, decent citizens banded together and decided that some of these people weren't really the victims of society that good progressive Berkeley likes to think they are. Suppose these good people decided that they were dealing with parasites, with individuals who would rather lay about all day, soak themselves in liquor or drugs, disrupt commerce, frighten mothers and children out of town, ruin the business of hardworking shopkeepers . . . ' Dr. Bernstein looked at her watch. 'I'm so sorry, Sergeant Plum, I have a class in ten minutes. I'll have to chase you out of my office now.'

Dr. Bernstein rested her hands on her desk and hoisted herself to her full height.

Marvia stood up. 'Wait a minute. Don't run off so quick.'

Bernstein shook her head. 'My students are waiting. You can walk with me if you wish.'

Dr. Bernstein, Dr. Chih and Marvia Plum started down the hallway. Bulletin boards were covered with want ads, course offerings, cut-rate travel offers.

Marvia raised her hands in front of her shoulders. 'Are you saying that a kind of — religious, quasi-religious cult is killing these people?'

'I don't know. But the different ways they died, the different suspicious figures who were reported afterwards — what does your police training tell you?'

'Huh! The patterns are different. Serials generally adopt a pet method and stick with it. Even professional hitters are usually self-consistent. We've had four incidents, five deaths, a different method each time.'

'Here's my session. Feel free at any time.' Dr. Bernstein shook Marvia's hand and disappeared into a crowded classroom. Dr. Chih shook Marvia's hand and headed off on a mission of her own.

Marvia walked south on Telegraph for a few blocks before heading west to police headquarters. The sun was sinking low and traffic was heavy. As Marvia neared People's Park she thought, *This is the time of day when they come out to play. The campfires will be burning, the crazies will be raving and the drug dealers will be making a fortune.*

It was also the time of day that squatters would be marking their territory in doorways and storefronts, setting up their little encampments and harassing shoppers foolish enough to stay on the avenue after dark.

But the avenue seemed more peaceful than usual for this hour. More shoppers remained on the streets, the cafés were brightly lit and crowded with students drinking coffee or beer, stores were staying open after dark again and they bustled with customers. Marvia wondered, *Where have all the loonies gone?*

She checked her watch as she started up the steps at headquarters. She hadn't been authorized any overtime for this job, and Lieutenant Yamura was a stickler for staying within budget.

There was a note on Marvia's desk. *Phone me at home, DY.* She punched Dorothy Yamura's private number.

'I had a call from Sally O'Hara in Chicago. They busted Parker Tice.'

'They have anything they can make stick?' Tice, Marvia Plum knew, was a top-flight hitter. Arrested many times, never convicted of anything worse than a couple of petty youth offenses.

'There was an Illinois warrant, I think they're going to squeeze hard this time. But that's up to the DA out there. But get this — Tice had an airline stub for a return flight from Oakland last Friday AM.'

'And Szymanski and Campbell got it Thursday night. And Tice is a shotgun specialist.'

'You got it.' Yamura spoke with a smile in her voice.

'You want me to fly out there?'

'Maybe later on. Not yet. Tice hates to talk to anybody, you know that. And we can't do anything on the strength of an airline stub. Keep working this end. This was just something I wanted you to know.'

Marvia hung up the phone and climbed into bed. She wasn't sure whether the phone rang just before or just after she had closed her eyes. It was Dorothy Yamura calling back.

'You're not going to believe this.'

'Unh?'

'Fredi Muhammad's dead.'

'Fredi? Feelgood Fredi, the biggest female dealer in the world of dope?'

'That's the one. And get this — she was sampling her own wares. I thought she was too smart for that, only the bottom-rungers do that. But she must have made a mistake, and it looks like the same stuff that killed LaTonia Jones.'

Marvia burrowed into her pillow, but the phone was still at her ear. 'Marvia?'

'Super-intense smack laced with strychnine?'

'You think it was an accident? Or was

somebody out to get Fredi?'

'I don't know, Marvia. Sweet dreams, sweetie. I'll talk to you tomorrow.'

★   ★   ★

In the morning, Marvia worked Telegraph again. She wore her uniform, gun and badge on display. Some citizens stood and gaped at her, others gave her a wide berth. Passing Woodstock West, she saw both Mistress Moonflower and Star Lotus inside the store. They wore similar outfits: filmy blouses and billowy skirts. Both were barefoot and wore jingling anklets. Moonflower was berating Star Lotus over something.

At the A-to-Z 24-Hour Market a mile south of campus, Marvia got lucky. A clerk remembered Otto Timmins. 'Poor old rummy,' was the way she put it. 'Never stopped talking about the navy. What war was he in, I guess Vietnam. Yeah, he used to talk about the Gulf of Tonkin and cruising on the Mekong Delta.'

'Why would anybody kill Timmins?' Marvia asked.

'Well, he was kind of obnoxious. I just felt sorry for him. But he smelled bad and he used to collar people with his war stories and then ask them for money. If they didn't give it to him he could get really hostile. Sometimes even if they did.'

'Just that?'

'And he used to scare children. He told me he loved them, but he used to lurch over and want to pet them or hug them and they'd scream and their mothers would hustle them out of his way. Manager made me bar him from the store but he just hung around outside panhandling and driving away customers. She said she didn't want to do it either, but the owner made her. You know, Cora Kelly? Big-time real estate operator, she owns a lot of places and has other people managing them for her. But I felt sorry for the guy. Poor old guy.'

Marvia laid a bill on the counter. 'Give me a cup of coffee, hey? Nice and hot.'

The clerk complied.

'When was the last time you saw Otto?'

'Well, it was the day before he was murdered. That's why I remember it. It was — ' She turned to a calendar with a picture of a female rock-climber perched triumphantly on top of Halfdome in Yosemite. The picture hung just below a big display clock with an advertising logo on it. The logo featured a blue dolphin drinking a stein of beer. ' — see, I pulled the graveyard shift that night, and I got home and climbed into bed and turned on the radio and there it was on the early morning news. So I thought, *Poor old Otto, poor old guy*. I know a lot of people figured, good riddance, but I thought, poor old guy.'

'What time did you see him, the day he was killed? Was he alone? Did he say or do anything you thought was unusual?'

'I remember there was a customer here, he started hassling her for money and I was going to throw him out but she made a gesture with her hand, like this, you know, like, it's okay, so I backed off.'

'What did she look like?'

'Slim build, sharp features, nice figure for an older woman. You know, slim, must be good genes, huh, look at me and I must be half her age.'

'Right. What else? Distinguishing marks, hair, clothing?'

'It was a chilly day. She was wearing a quilted vest, I remember that. And her hair — looked like steel wool. I never saw hair like that before. Must feel really interesting. Kind of a turn-on.'

'Anything else? What did they do? What did they say to each other? Did they leave together?'

'That's it. He asked her for money and she stopped and looked at him, I remember that. I mean, people didn't like to look at Otto. He was a little too weird, you know? Just — not nice, that's all. But this woman looked at him, and she leaned over and said something in his ear, and she walked out of the store. And Otto stood there, I remember, looking at the clock and moving his lips, like he was counting the time. Then he grunted something like, 'Okay, it's time,' and he went out of the store.'

Marvia sat on a bench outside the A-to-Z making notes in her pocket notebook. The woman with steel-wool hair . . . that hair was Ceejay Harker's trademark. And Ceejay

was one of the country's top female hitters. No, that wasn't it. She was one of the
country's top hitters, gender of no concern. She was a woman of a certain age
— the records disagreed on what that age
was — and she stood at the top of her
field.

Had Parker Tice shotgunned Bill
Szymanski and Robin Campbell, and
Ceejay Harker put a .22 slug into the base
of Otto Timmins' skull? Two top hitters
for two trash-level hits? Did that make
sense? But if that was the case, then what
about LaTonia Jones and Fredi Muhammad? Was that just a coincidence, or was
that killing — make it those killings,
now — connected with the Szymanski-
Campbell and Timmins incidents?

Maybe it was just a coincidence, but
Dorothy Yamura was famous for her dis-
like of coincidences. They made her nervous,
she said, and she drilled it into her sub-
ordinates not to trust coincidence, but to
look for the underlying connection.

Marvia Plum walked back on Telegraph.
Near Woodstock West she ran into Star
Lotus. The young woman was in tears.

When she spotted Marvia she started to turn away, then spun around — Marvia could see she was wearing low-top boots, at least she wasn't walking the street barefoot — and ran toward Marvia.

She was running past Marvia when Marvia reached out and caught her by the arms. 'What's the matter? What happened?'

Star Lotus looked at Marvia and shook her head. Her cheeks were wet. The smell of too-sweet incense came off her clothing, mixed with the sharpness of cannabis and the reek of hashish. 'That — that — she fired me.'

'Why?' Marvia frowned.

'I can't tell you.'

'Sure you can.' Marvia put her arm around Star Lotus's shoulders. 'Come on, we'll find someplace quiet. You can talk to me.' *So now I'm a social worker*, she thought. *Or maybe an employment counselor. Well, all in a day's work.*

Caffe Brasil was jammed to the gills, but Marvia Plum's uniform helped them find a table. The customers were a mix of older students, faculty, working people and shoppers. A few stared at Marvia's uniform. She ignored them. She was used to it. When the waiter arrived Star Lotus asked for a glass of wine. The waiter looked at Marvia, then asked Star Lotus for ID. She fumbled for a wallet and showed a card. The waiter nodded, looking sheepish. 'I have to ask. Joanna's a real stickler for that. You know, Joanna Moreira, the owner.'

Marvia said, 'Cappuccino.' If she didn't die of caffeine poisoning, she was certainly living by it.

'I wouldn't do what she told me,' Star Lotus said. Her glass of wine had arrived and to Marvia Plum's amazement she'd chug-a-lugged it. She looked around frantically, caught the waiter's eye and waved her empty glass. The waiter disappeared to get her another.

'Take it easy,' Marvia suggested. 'Did you eat today? Are you drinking that stuff on an empty stomach?'

'I don't care.' By the time they entered the café Star Lotus had stopped crying but now she started again. She used a napkin to dab her eyes and wipe her cheeks. The tears had made tracks there in her makeup. Marvia could see that, under the makeup, she had a serious complexion problem.

Marvia sipped her cappuccino. 'You wouldn't do what Mistress Moonflower wanted, so she fired you?'

Star Lotus nodded. The waiter set her second glass of wine on the table in front of her with one hand, removing the empty with the other. Star Lotus picked up the second glass and took a big sip, but at least she didn't finish the glass this time. 'The — the — I shouldn't have done it the first time.'

'What did she want you to do?'

'You remember that old lady, that Imaculata?'

'Imaculata Martinez. She the one?'

'She used to sell things to us. Try and sell them. Just junk. She was a trash picker, you know. She used to find things in the trash, broken earrings, junk, you know. And she'd try and sell them to us. At first we used to give her a little money, I felt sorry for her, I guess Moonflower did too. We'd give her a little money for

41

the things she brought in and then we'd throw them away.'

She paused and took another slug of wine.

'Moonflower got tired of it after a while and told her not to come around any more, she was bothering the customers. You know, most of our customers are young kids, they're embarrassed to be in the store buying incense and rolling papers and condoms and things. And they didn't like being around Imaculata, so they'd go to another store or whatever. But she kept coming around anyhow, and Moonflower told me — '

Marvia grabbed Star Lotus's wrist. 'Stop!'

Star Lotus jumped. 'What's the matter?'

'Don't say another word. Listen here.' She unbuttoned the pocket on her uniform shirt and pulled out a Miranda card. She read the lines to Star Lotus. She knew the Miranda warning by heart, but Dorothy Yamura insisted that her people read it anyhow, every time, just to be safe. When she finished she said, 'I want you to come with me.'

Star Lotus said, 'Where? Don't make

me go back. I'm afraid of her, I don't want to go back there.'

'To Woodstock West? We're not going there.'

'Where are we going?'

'Are you carrying a concealed weapon?' Star Lotus shook her head. 'Do you want to walk? I'll call for a unit if you want. Would you rather ride?'

'Ride? Wha — ?'

'Will you go with me to police headquarters, Star Lotus? Will you go voluntarily and talk with me there?'

Star Lotus stood up. Marvia Plum dropped another bill on the table. She took Star Lotus by one wrist. She didn't handcuff her. She started away from the table, Star Lotus in tow. Star Lotus picked up her half-full glass of wine and emptied it before they reached the door. She placed it on the shelf just inside the door before following Marvia Plum back onto Telegraph.

At police headquarters Marvia Plum put Star Lotus in an interrogation room, then fetched Dorothy Yamura. On the way back from Yamura's office she briefed the lieutenant on Star Lotus's statement at the café. Dorothy Yamura asked if Marvia had mirandized Star Lotus. Even though she had done so, Dorothy Yamura insisted on doing it again, with a tape running and in the presence of both a public defender and an assistant DA.

The PD advised Star Lotus to say nothing until they'd conferred in private, but Star Lotus insisted on telling her story. 'She made me,' Star Lotus sobbed. 'She said I had to do it.'

The assistant DA laid a sympathetic hand on Star Lotus's hand. 'Do what, dear? Made you do what?'

'She made me take that poor old lady, that Mrs. Martinez, over to What's Flat and Round with a Hole in the Middle, you know, the big record store. She said I had to take her into the bathroom and stab her. It was the only way to get rid of her. She was ruining our business and we couldn't get rid of her any other way. We called the police and sometimes they wouldn't even come at all, and other times they'd say they couldn't do anything, we were open to the public and she was a member of the public.'

'But I don't understand,' the assistant DA put in. Star Lotus wiped her eyes and looked up at the woman. Marvia Plum thought, this assistant DA was really good. She was about to unleash the *Please help me, dear*, ploy, Marvia was certain.

'Please help me, dear,' the assistant DA said, 'how could she make you kill someone? You did kill Mrs. Martinez, didn't you?'

The PD was about to have a hissy-fit, but Star Lotus was clearly in the unburdening mode, and there was no stopping her now.

'I ran away from home. I didn't have anything. I was getting into a lot of trouble, I knew it. I was hanging around with bad people. I lived in the park for a while myself. Strangers were coming on to me, you know, coming on to me. And everybody was either getting drunk or smoking crack or shooting up, and one person grabbed me one time and tried to take me away and sell me. Sell me!'

She stopped to catch her breath. She

asked for a glass of water and Marvia Plum sent a uniform to get it for her.

The assistant DA said, 'How did you meet Mistress Moonflower?'

Star Lotus squeezed her eyes shut as if she was looking inside herself for a memory. 'I was panhandling. I went into Woodstock West to try and get some money, and she said she wouldn't give me a handout but I could try out for a job there. She said I was really pretty, and people liked to buy things from you if you were pretty.'

She looked around at all the others, the assistant DA, the PD, Lieutenant Yamura and Sergeant Plum and the uniform who had returned with a glass of water. The uniform handed the glass to Star Lotus. She took it and said, 'Thanks,' and took a deep drink and set the glass down in front of her. She wiped her eyes and swept her hair back from her face and licked her lips to give them a moist look.

'I am pretty, don't you think? Everybody always says I'm pretty.'

The assistant DA said, 'Yes, Star Lotus, you're pretty. Is that your real name, Star

46

Lotus? That isn't your real name, is it?'

Star Lotus shook her head. 'Moon-flower changed my name. It used to be Anna Mae Jenkins. Moonflower said, if I was going to work at Woodstock West, I had to have the right kind of name, and wear the right kind of clothes, and act kind of — kind of like one of those old, uh, I think she called them hippie chicks. That's what she said I had to be, a hippie chick.'

The assistant DA said, 'How old are you, Anna Mae?'

'Twenty-one. I have ID. I showed it to the waiter at Caffe Brasil, didn't I, Sergeant Plum? Right? It's still right here, right?'

The assistant DA turned the card over. She squinted at it, turned it over again. 'Nice job. How old are you really, Anna Mae?'

'I'm really — '

'Please, dear, we want to help you.'

The PD looked as if she was about to pop a blood vessel.

'I'm 15.' Beneath the bright interrogation-room light, Anna Mae Jenkins' face took on a peculiar look; she might be 15 or she might be twice that age. 'I was always big for my age, and I matured early. There were always boys after me and I didn't know what to do. I didn't like it, but they always said, Yes, I really did like it, I didn't know what I really liked. I got so confused. And my father used to — he used to — back in Tennessee, I'm originally from Tennessee, did you know that?'

She looked up and smiled, showing her teeth.

The assistant DA and the PD exchanged a few quiet words. Then the assistant DA said, 'This is all wrong. This child belongs with the juvenile authorities, not here. My God, but she needs help.'

Dorothy Yamura said, 'Come along, Anna Mae. You can sit in my office. You can wait there and we'll get somebody to take you someplace safe.'

Anna Mae said, 'Really?'

Dorothy Yamura nodded.

Anna Mae said, 'Really safe? Really?'

'Really safe, Anna Mae.'

And a little later, Lieutenant Yamura talked with Sergeant Plum. 'Marvia, I

48

don't know what to say. I should be furious, you let a 15-year-old child fool you into thinking she was 21. But she fooled me, so I guess I can't be too hard on you.'

'I feel rotten about it.' Marvia put her fingertips against her temples and rubbed, trying to ease a sudden headache. 'But I know what we have to do.'

'You bet. Back to Woodstock West. We've got a date with — what did you say Mistress Moonflower's real name was?'

'Myrna Gersh.'

'Myrna Gersh.'

Mistress Moonflower had wasted no time in replacing Star Lotus. Marvia Plum went through the front door of Woodstock West while a couple of uniforms stationed themselves at the back door.

A new hippie chick was behind the counter, waiting on a customer while Mistress Moonflower supervised. The new hippie chick had long, glossy hair parted in the middle and hanging down the back of her floor-length, Hindu-patterned dress. She wore yellow-tinted, Janis Joplin glasses, a nose-ring, and brass bangles up one arm.

Incense rose from a hammered-brass burner on the glass counter, as if carrying prayers past the Jimi Hendrix icon on the wall behind.

The new hippie chick look startled when Marvia entered the shop, but Mistress Moonflower smiled her sour smile at Marvia and said, 'Sergeant Plum, this is my new helper, Amber Glow.'

Marvia said, 'Okay, Amber Glow, shoo the customer out and lock up. I'm afraid Woodstock West is closing. Myrna, you have the right to remain silent. You are not required to say anything . . . '

Myrna Gersh's first reaction was to brazen it out, but by the time the assistant DA had finished playing Anna Mae Jenkins' tape for her she was willing to cut a deal. She wasn't in it alone. Joanna Moreira, Cora Kelly, half the merchants on Telegraph Avenue were in it with her.

The drug dealers, the panhandlers, the crazies and the child molesters in the park, the doorway squatters and the sidewalk campers and the common thugs were destroying business on the avenue. They were ruining the town, and the town would pay an even greater price when its already slipping commercial tax base shrank to zero.

Then who would pay the police officers' salaries?

Then who would pay for the politicians' perks?

The government refused to clean up the city, the politicians practically invited vagrants and parasites to join the party.

The merchants had to act, and they had hired hitters, one by one, to come to town and removed the most flagrant nuisances. There was no one Tallyman. The Tallyman had been Parker Tice, he had been Ceejay Harker, he had been Fredi Muhammad. It was true that using poor bewildered Anna Mae Jenkins, a.k.a. Star Lotus, to remove Imaculata Martinez had been a serious mistake, but if they had it all to do over again . . .

Within days, not only Myrna Gersh but half a dozen other entrepreneurs were in custody. The charges ranged from conspiracy to capital murder. Bail was denied to each defendant.

Two weeks later the assistant DA sat

in Lieutenant Yamura's office along with Sergeant Plum. The DA said, 'I don't know what we're going to do about this. Have you been following the public reaction to the Tallyman case?'

Lieutenant Yamura closed the lid on a palmtop computer she'd been consulting and placed it carefully in a desk drawer. 'You bet I have. Most of the editorials were on our side.'

'At first,' the assistant DA put in.

'At first, yes. Then the talk shows started going nuts all over the area. And the letter columns. Have you looked at the Oakland *Trib* lately, or the Berkeley *Voice*? Even the *Express* is starting to come around.'

'Come around against us, you mean.'

'That's exactly what I mean.'

'There's a Tallyman Society on the university campus. There are at least a dozen people going around town claiming to be the Tallyman, and everybody wants to buy 'em a meal or a drink. On my way over here today I saw four or five cars with *Tallyman for Mayor* bumper stickers, and one that said, *Honk if you love the Tallyman* and people were honking, believe me.'

'What are you going to do?' Dorothy Yamura asked.

The assistant DA shrugged her shoulders. 'I don't know. Maybe go for a change of venue.'

Marvia Plum asked, 'Isn't that usually a defense tactic?'

The DA nodded. 'Usually, sister, that's right. Usually.'

'I had a phone call from Dr. Chih this morning,' Marvia told the others. 'She says that business is still up on the avenue. The crime rate is dropping. We know that, of course, as well as she does or better. A couple of businesses have closed up, but others are eager to move in. It looks as if Telly is turning around. At least, so Dr. Chih says.'

Dorothy Yamura turned to Marvia Plum. 'I don't want to keep you here longer than necessary, Sergeant. I know you have plenty of work to do.'

'I have,' Marvia Plum admitted. 'I surely have.' She left the meeting and went back to her job.

2

Black Boy in a Box

'I don't think so. I don't work narco. Never have.'

'I know that. I have your record right here.'

'Well, then.'

'Besides, I've known you for your whole career.'

'Well, then.'

'Tell me why you feel this way, Marvia. You're one of my best people. You're a fine detective. You have a great arrest record and an outstanding conviction rate. Why don't you want this assignment?'

Sergeant Marvia Plum shifted in her chair. It wasn't just that Lieutenant Yamura was her boss. If anything, that would have made it easier. Keep things objective, professional. Don't let your feelings get control. But it wasn't that way. Lieutenant Yamura was her friend

54

and had been her sponsor in the Berkeley Police Department, had coaxed her into the job to start with, and had pushed her promotion to sergeant.

More, Dorothy Yamura had helped her get her job and her stripes back when she'd resigned from the force to marry and move out of state, and then returned with an annulment in one pocket and a restraining order against her new ex in the other.

'Look, Dorothy, I've got a twelve-year-old. He asks me why it's okay for me to have a drink after work. And he wants to know why it's okay for TV stars to smoke cigarettes and baseball players to chew tobacco, but a high school kid can get busted for smoking a joint. And I have a hard time answering him.'

Dorothy sighed. 'It's the law.'

Marvia shook her head. 'I tell him that. The law is the law. But he just turns off. And I don't blame him.'

'So you don't want to work narco.'

Marvia nodded. She wouldn't refuse the assignment if Dorothy Yamura made it an order, but short of that, she hoped she could argue her way out of it or plead her way out of it. She'd much rather work on a nice juicy murder.

But Dorothy Yamura wasn't biting. 'We're not talking about high school kids smoking a little pot, Marvia. We're talking about bad, bad stuff. We're talking about crack and smack and ice. And we're pretty sure that the stuff is going through the Crash Club.'

'Okay.' Marvia touched the corner of her badge, as if subconsciously afraid that it wouldn't be there. 'Just raid the place.'

'You're kidding. We'd have a riot. Hundreds of university students, slumming yuppies, you know the kind of trashing we'd take in the city council?'

'Who owns the club?'

'Solomon San Remo.'

'Saintly Solly?'

'The very.'

'I thought he was running some kind of real estate scam. You sure we're talking about the same leading citizen?'

'Yes.'

Marvia caught a glimpse of herself, reflected in the glass fronting on a citation hanging on the wall behind Dorothy Yamura's desk. Short, black hair. Dark complexion, heavy bones, a generous figure that required a constant struggle to keep under control. Her Berkeley police uniform was immaculate, although she knew she'd work in civvies if she worked a narco case.

'Last I knew, Solly was running a youth rehab center on University Avenue. Pulling in funds all over the place — federal, state, city, private donors, do-gooder foundations. What's he doing running a nightclub?'

'You know Solly. He managed to live high and sock away a fat retirement fund for himself, bought up a nice parcel of real estate on University, announced the ground-breaking for his project.'

Yamura paused. Marvia Plum waited for her to go on, and finally she did.

'Wouldn't you know, the whole thing just never quite happened. The neighbors started hollering NIMBY. Everybody was in favor of a rehab center, but *Not In My Back Yard!* They got their city council member — who had been one hundred per cent in favor of San Remo and his good works — to fight *against* it when it came up for a vote. You know the buzzwords. Dangerous characters roaming the streets, school children and old people getting mugged or worse, send these troubled individuals off to the wholesome air of the countryside someplace.'

'I get it,' Marvia put in. 'So there was Solomon San Remo with all that real estate and nothing to build on it.'

'Right.' Yamura stood up and studied some papers held onto a file cabinet with superhero magnets. Marvia Plum recognized Mary Marvel and Supergirl and Wonder Woman. 'Guess I don't need my invitation to a retirement party three weeks ago. A free pass to a movie that closed last month.' She pulled a few scraps from beneath the magnets and dropped them in her wastebasket.

'So now he wants to put up a couple of condo's on the land. Take him years to pull that deal together and get it through all the boards and commissions. But in the meanwhile he wound up owning the Crash Club and he's kept it open because it generates a nice little cash flow for him.'

Marvia Plum let the heel of her hand rest on the grip of the 9 mm. Glock resting in a holster on her hip. She'd got so accustomed to carrying a piece in her years on the Berkeley force, she'd felt half-naked without it when she moved to Nevada. It was a comfort to have it back.

She said, 'Who's dealing the dope at San Remo's club?'

Yamura looked stolidly at Marvia. 'I don't know.'

'Have we talked to Solly? Is he cooperating? If we can show criminal activity at his club, even if he isn't involved, unless he exercises due diligence he can lose his license.'

'That's just it. We think Solly himself is behind it. Either he's looking the other way, letting the pushers do their work, and taking *baksheesh* for his kindness — or he's actively involved.'

'What do our sources say?'

'Nothing. Nada. Nix. You have to get past Solly's personal door dragon to get into the club, and he's got a sharp eye. Seems as if he knows all the regular junkies and speed freaks in town, won't let 'em inside the place. And a real terror on ID. Crash Club caters to UC students, twenty-something's, yuppies. We can't even get an underage kid in there to bust 'em for selling liquor.'

Marvia Plum lowered her face into her hands and pressed against her eyelids. Flashes of light went off inside her eyes. Images of past busts, trials, funerals. 'Okay.' She raised her head. 'Okay, Dorothy. What's our strategy?'

Dorothy Yamura briefed Marvia on the plan for taking down the operation at the Crash Club. When she finished talking, Marvia stood up and turned to leave Yamura's office. Dorothy stopped her with a word. 'Marvia.'

Plum turned around and waited.

'Marvia,' Yamura repeated, 'What convinced you?'

Marvia managed a weak smile. 'You know I'm a realist, Dorothy. I don't believe in ghosts or visions or ESP or UFO's or any other hooey. I go to church once in a while, but that's not belief, it's desperation.'

Yamura raised her eyebrows. She was in uniform today, her creases razor-sharp and her lieutenant's insignia glistening in the cold glare of fluorescents. She waited for Marvia to get to the point.

She did. 'I had a little vision. Something like old Scrooge and the Spirit of Christmas Yet-to-Come.' She shuddered and rubbed her hands against the sleeves of her woolen uniform blouse; the friction gave her a little warmth. 'I saw my boy in a box. Is it too late, Spirit? Can I change this, Spirit? I'll do anything it takes, Dorothy.'

* * *

The Crash Club was on the north side of University Avenue, less than a mile from the UC campus. The doors opened at 9:00 PM, and the first band wasn't scheduled to play until 11:00. Marvia Plum had checked out and gone home for a quiet nap and a light meal before making her rendezvous a few blocks from the club.

Time was, time had been, when she

could have worked a full day, stayed up most of the night on a stakeout and gone back to work after a shower and breakfast. Right. And time had been when she could party all night and keep on going the next morning, too.

She wondered if she could pass for young enough to patronize the Crash Club.

She was teamed with Evangeline Rhee. Marvia had known Vangie for years, knew that she had worked deep cover for the DEA before she got disgusted with the agency's tactics and her boss's high-handed attitude and resigned. No explosion, no confrontation, that wouldn't have been Vangie's way. A quiet, dignified letter of resignation, and a new job at the local cop-shop.

Vangie had started life as a forensic photographer. She knew everything there was to know about lenses and shutter speeds, apertures and emulsions. Moving from that role into undercover work had brought her out of the lab and into the world of hitters and snatchers, bagmen and mules. Her later hiring by the BPD was done quietly and she pursued a public career as a celebrity photog, a member of the paparazzi gang who would turn up at everything from opening night at the San Francisco Opera to opening day at the Oakland Coliseum. She sold photos to the *Chronicle*, the *Examiner*, the *Trib*, the *Express* and the San Francisco *Mirror*.

And she got into backstage scenes, dressing rooms and locker rooms and smoke-filled rooms (there were still a few of those) and provided reports to the Berkeley PD Intelligence Unit that had put more than one fence, kink, or sleaze-bag into San Quentin, Soledad, or Pelican Bay. It was risky work, and she knew that if her cover were blown she'd be lucky to get out alive.

She loved it.

Dorothy Yamura had told Marvia that there would be a couple of male plainclothes officers in the crowd at the Crash Club, and a 'tac squad ready to close in if needed. That was the good news. But the officers going inside would be unarmed. The Crash Club's bouncer/

manager, 'Chuff' Fernandez, had installed a metal detector just inside the club's doorway. No guns, no knives, no weapons in the club.

It was a good idea. Nobody could complain about that, not even City Councilmember Sherry Hanson, last of the red-hot radicals. She considered the police department a pack of fascist pigs and Marvia Plum a traitor to her race, her gender, and her class.

The detector kept weapons out of the club. It also meant that the police couldn't carry their normal equipment with them without giving themselves away.

Marvia had raised that question, and Dorothy Yamura had said, 'We can't risk it. If Solly is in cahoots with the pushers — or if Chuff Fernandez is — and we clear our presence in advance, there's no way we'll catch anything. The support will be outside, that's the best I can offer.'

Now Marvia and Vangie stood on the sidewalk outside the Crash Club.

They were surrounded by celebrants of varied persuasions. Most of the line was composed of young people, and it was moving, up ahead. Red and blue neon made garish patterns on the customers. Some got past Chuff Fernandez and disappeared beneath the Crash Club's neon logo. Others too young to pass muster were turned away. Some tried to argue the point, but Fernandez never yielded.

Ahead of Marvia and Vangie were a couple with spiked Mohawks, the taller partner's hair dyed a vivid green; the shorter partner's, a rich maroon. They wore identical black biker's jackets and silver chains running from their ears to their nostrils.

The line lurched and Marvia felt a shove from behind. She turned and saw that the person behind her was apparently alone. Not that it mattered: he was big enough for a party of four. His skull was completely hairless but he sported a bushy iron-gray beard. His forehead had a single word tattooed on it: TOD. Drops of blood — Marvia realized they were simulated — ran from the letters and disappeared into the man's eyes. He wore a long-sleeved shirt with fancy embroidery at the cuffs: braid like the decoration on an army officer's dress uniform, with a grinning dinosaur peeking between the loops. At least the strange man had a sense of humor.

Outside the Crash Club, what looked like a onetime church announcement board had been adapted to list the night's attractions. *Hitler Youth . . . Smutnik . . . PRYZN GYRLS.*

The line reached the door. Marvia had the price of admission in her hand but Vangie Rhee held up her camera with one hand and her press pass with the other. She was testing a new electronic camera tonight, courtesy of the San Francisco *Mirror.* A combination camcorder and minicomputer, it would allegedly store an image on a silicon chip instead of a piece of celluloid and display the image on a rectangular screen without benefit of chemicals.

Chuff Fernandez nodded at Vangie. Vangie pointed over her shoulder at Marvia. Chuff grabbed Marvia by her biceps and propelled her inside the club. He was dark-skinned, darker even than Marvia. His shirt had a Cuban flag on it.

He didn't say a word.

At least she'd got through the metal detector with her badge in her pocket. Not enough metal in it to set off an alarm. She might not be able to apply deadly force, but if it came down to it she might accomplish something with moral force.

Sure.

The club was already jammed. If the BPD or the ABC didn't close it down, Marvia thought, then the Fire Marshal ought to give it a try.

The bands had brought out their respective followings, and Marvia played a silent game, identifying patrons by their musical taste. It was easy enough to pick out Hitler Youth's fans — skinheads, some of them in T-shirts and jeans, some in pseudo-military attire. Swastika necklaces and sneering faces and lots of bad complexions. Smutnik fans wore death-white makeup and black clothes, black hair and black lipstick. There were even a few black Smutniks with deep white sockets painted around their eyes to simulate death.

And PRYZN GYRLZ seemed to draw lesbian couples. When a pair drew near one of them put an arm across Marvia's chest and leaned her mouth against her ear. Her breath was hot and moist. She said, 'Ditch the white bitch, honey, what's the matter with you?'

Marvia shook free. 'We're just friends,' she managed.

The two PRYZN GYRLZ fans traded looks and nods. They were both wearing PRYZN GYRLZ T-shirts. 'Sure, honey. Just don't waste it. Come on over and have a drink.' They headed for the bar.

Marvia looked at Vangie.

Vangie's eyes lit up as if she'd seen an old friend and she disappeared into the crowd.

Marvia and her new friends fought through the crush to reach the bar. Somehow they succeeded. Marvia found herself with a new friend on either side. Two black women, both of them in sweat-stained T-shirts. Marvia wore a sweatshirt, its sleeves chopped at the shoulders. She missed the familiar weight of a piece on her hip or in a shoulder holster. The bar was darkwood, had a real brass rail, a huge mirror on the wall behind the bartenders. Clearly, the heritage of some earlier incarnation of the Crash Club.

One of Marvia's new friends yelled at a female bartender. She slapped a bill onto the wood. The bartender drew three beers into plastic cups and set them on the wood. There was a stack of paper napkins printed with the Crash Club's logo, a huge, ancient Buick convertible wrapped around a tree.

The woman to Marvia's left raised her glass and said, 'To us, honey.' They all drank. Marvia took as little beer as she could; it wasn't the old drinking-on-duty taboo, she just needed to keep her wits as sharp and her reflexes as fast as she could.

The club was already dark, Marvia thought, when she came past Chuff Fernandez. Now it got darker. A spotlight hit a man standing on the stage. Marvia recognized Solomon San Remo, but just barely. He'd been a heavyset man when she'd known him — or known of him — in the past. She hadn't seen him for a long time, not since a couple of years before she moved to Nevada and not since she'd moved back. Now he looked emaciated. He wore his iron gray hair in a ponytail and a hippie-style headband straight out of the Summer of Love.

He announced the first band.

Hitler Youth pounded and screamed at the audience. They wore fatigue caps with death's head insignia and they flashed Nazi salutes. The audience shifted like a giant organism. By osmosis, skinheads moved toward the stage. They returned the salutes and shouted. 'Sieg heil! Sieg heil! Sieg heil!'

The room seemed to grow hotter. Marvia was sweating. She realized this was no illusion. The body heat of a couple of hundred young, sweating, jumping humans could raise the temperature to any level. One of Marvia's new friends had her arm around her shoulder.

Marvia said, 'I have to — ' She left the sentence hanging. She'd put her beer back on the wood. She headed for the bathroom. She managed to squeeze into the room. It was as crowded as the club itself. She smelled a too-familiar odor, pungent and slightly sweet. Somebody was passing a joint around. She didn't care. She was looking for bigger game. The city council had ordered the police to give marijuana offenses the lowest possible priority anyway, lower than throwing gum wrappers in the street, and she wasn't going to waste her time on a weed bust.

She squeezed into a stall and relieved herself and headed back to the floor. Hitler Youth was taking an encore. An ancient advertising clock shaped like a DeSoto sedan showed that they'd played for forty minutes. Marvia didn't know about that. For a while there it had seemed as if they'd been pounding and howling for centuries.

A fight broke out between a skinhead and a fat white woman in a PRYZN GYRLZ T-shirt. From nowhere, a squad of bouncers appeared and surrounded the fighters. Marvia recognized Chuff Fernandez among them, giving directions. In seconds the skinhead was out of sight, the woman returned to her friends. It was as if nothing had happened.

Marvia was at the edge of the stage. From her perspective she could see into the wings on the opposite side. There wasn't much room there, but some paparazzi were crammed into a few square feet of space. Marvia recognized Vangie Rhee, her classic Korean features distinctive.

For a moment Vangie looked down into the audience and Marvia caught her eye and nodded. Vangie made a gesture with her head.

A figure emerged from the shadows on the far end of the stage and Solomon San Remo walked to the microphone and announced Smutnik.

They were less abrasive than Hitler Youth. The Nazi wanna-be's drifted away from the stage. Maybe they were leaving the club, headed off to meetings somewhere to practice goose-stepping or read selections from *Mein Kampf*. Smutnik played a kind of slow, pulsing dirge. A singer slithered up to the microphone and mumbled monotonous lyrics in an androgynous voice.

The audience took its signal from the band, swaying slowly, looking as if they were interested only in slow, dreamy oblivion.

The skinheads had been candidates for ice, for crank, for whatever form of speed was this year's charted hit. Hitler himself, Marvia had learned, liked uppers. Cocaine had been the drug of choice in the *Fuhrer-bunker*. Smutnik fans were a different breed. They would go for reds, booze, Quaaludes, ecstasy.

If anybody came to the club stoned, there was no way the police could control that. Marvia would have staked a week's pay that half the audience, at least, had some form of illegal substance in their bloodstream. But there had been no evidence of pushing in the Crash Club. At this rate, the night's efforts were going to come up with a fat nothing.

Marvia drifted through the club. The wall opposite the bar was covered with a mural left over from an earlier era. She recognized some of the faces from her childhood. She and her brother, Tyrone, had been too young to participate fully in the Sixties phenomenon, but living in Berkeley they had been exposed to all of the controversy and all of the euphoria of that brief, colorful era.

There was Jimi Hendrix, there was Janis Joplin, there were Mama Cass Elliot, Jim Morrison, Jerry Garcia. All of them dead. All of them victims.

The powder flowed, the needles gleamed, the crack pipes glowed and still they died. They never learned.

She thought of a black boy in a box.

She saw a familiar face, recognized a Berkeley cop in beard and army fatigues. He was dancing with another Berkeley cop. The bearded officer locked eyes with Marvia, nodded, gestured toward the stage with his head.

Smutnik was off the stage and Solomon San Remo was giving the featured band of the evening a big buildup. Women were crowding toward the stage, some of them yelling at San Remo and gesturing at him, urging him off the stage. He took the hint and disappeared.

PRYZN GYRLZ charged onto the stage.

Their fans cheered as if nothing else in the universe mattered.

The band leaped into their first

number, the drummer pounding at her drum-kit, the bass player thundering deep notes, the guitarist making her instrument screech and wail. Marvia felt tears of pain come to her eyes.

The leader of the band was a tall, bony young woman with vaguely Asian features. She clutched a cordless mike, panted into it, rubbed it on her body. She used the stage name Apryl Pyzn, Marvia knew from her briefing.

The PRYZN GYRLZ fans jumped and chanted.

Apryl Pyzn retreated to the back of the stage. There wasn't much room. The singer ran full-tilt to the front of the stage and launched herself into the air.

A dozen arms emerged from the crowd and caught her. She was passed across the heads of the crowd, the microphone still in her hand, holding it to one ecstatic fan after another, to add a word or a phrase to the song. The rest of PRYZN GYRLZ stayed on the stage, working their instruments to the max.

The singer came within inches of Marvia. She saw the woman, her face covered with perspiration, her expression entranced. An arm came up from the crowd. Marvia couldn't see who wore it but she recognized part of a shirt-sleeve, an odd cuff with gold braid and a grinning dinosaur. And she saw something else. She saw something flash toward Apryl Pyzn's leg, then disappear back into the crowd. At the same moment she saw a flash from the stage wings, as bright and brief as a photographer's flashbulb.

Something else appeared in Apryl Pyzn's face: surprise; and then she was gone, surfing across the crowd, handed back toward the stage and pushed upright.

She looked around. Marvia spotted Vangie Rhee in the wings, shooting the stage and the audience. Then Apryl Pyzn looked pleased, then she dropped the cordless microphone and slumped to the stage.

Women in the front of the room started screaming. The bass player and guitarist dropped their instruments and ran to Apryl. The drummer, absorbed in her music, pounded away for thirty seconds that seemed like a month before she looked up from her drum-kit, stopped playing, dropped her sticks and tried to run straight toward Apryl, forgetting that the floor-mounted bass drum and top-hat cymbals were between them. The drums and cymbals crashed to the stage. A heavy brass disk bounced once and then crashed into the crowd.

Marvia grabbed the undercover officer she had spotted earlier, yelled, 'Get out, get backup,' and headed for the stage. She held her badge in a red-gel spotlight and shouted. 'Everyone stay calm. Turn on the house-lights. No one leave, the club is surrounded by police officers.'

There was a stir in the crowd as the fat man with TOD tattooed on his forehead tried to escape from the crowd but he moved too late. He reached the club's stage door and ran into the arms of half a dozen Berkeley police officers.

★　★　★

Sergeant Marvia Plum and Detective Evangeline Rhee sat in Dorothy Yamura's office; the man with TOD tattooed on his forehead sat in a conference room nearby, talking earnestly with his lawyer. The man with TOD tattooed on his forehead looked dramatically different than he had at the Crash Club. The blood-red word and the simulated drops of blood were gone, washed clean after he had been photographed by police ID techs.

More, he looked oddly shrunken. The belly was gone. His T-shirt hung loose around his torso and his jeans would have fallen off if he hadn't held them up. If it hadn't been for his heavy beard, he could have passed for the brother of Solomon San Remo.

Dorothy Yamura gazed levelly at Marvia Plum and Vangie Rhee. 'I thought I'd heard everything, but this one is new to me. The fake tattoos weren't a big surprise, I've seen perps before who put on some bizarre garment or wig to distract attention from their faces, so the tattoo makes sense. Grisly sense of humor, though. *Tod*.'

'I thought that was his name,' Marvia put in, 'or maybe the name of a lost love.'

'That would be Todd with two d's. Tod with one d is German for Death. And that's what he was peddling. Good thing your new little camera works, Vangie.'

Computer-generated blowups of the key frames Vangie had shot during Apryl Pyzn's final crowd-surf lay on her desk. In one of them the tell-tale embroidered sleeve was visible. From it protruded a hand holding a hypodermic needle, about to plunge it into Apryl Pyzn's leg.

'But that fake belly . . . where do you think he got the idea for that?'

'Some movie,' Evangeline put in. 'They send stills to us at the *Mirror* and the other papers all the time. They can make a fake anything now, that you can hardly tell from a real one. Including a big roly-poly belly.'

'And Tod — or whatever his real name is — carried his stock of poison inside the fake belly. In the Crash Club it was easy to deliver his drugs and collect cash. Dark, crowded, the place was full of odd characters, most of them anonymous. As for killing Apryl Pyzn — we're still checking her background, and the rest of

PRYZN GYRLZ, but I expect we'll learn that Tod was their supplier and he got into some kind of fight with Apryl. She wouldn't pay her bills, or he'd been delivering bad merchandise, or — whatever. We'll find out. I expect the other PRYZN GYRLZ will be happy to cut a deal and get Tod sent away forever if not longer.'

Dorothy Yamura allowed herself one of her rare smiles. 'You think you could work narco again, Marvia?'

Marvia didn't answer at once. She was thinking of her son, in bed and asleep now. She thought of him in the daylight, running, laughing, alive.

3

That Little Toy is Lost

Eric Coffman was in court in Martinez when Hobart Lindsey's jet touched down at Oakland International, but Miriam Coffman was at the airport in the family station wagon. She wouldn't think of dropping Lindsey at a motel, and if she even tried it there would be no living with Eric. Of course Lindsey was going to accept a ride to the house, and sit down at the dinner table, and stay over in the spare bedroom for as long as he was in town.

And there was no saying no to the comfortable, pleasant-mannered, iron-willed Miriam Coffman.

Hours later, over coffee and brandy and a soothing Mendelssohn sonata, Lindsey's years away from California dissipated and the warmth of an old friendship returned and filled the cozy living room.

Eric was using his best lawyerly

listening skills and Lindsey was just beginning to open up about his recent adventures when the phone rang. Eric Coffman lifted the cordless phone and without speaking handed it to Lindsey.

'Why aren't you on the job? What are you doing at your pal's house, gobbling brie and quaffing liebfraumilch?'

'No, we — '

'Never mind. Lace up your shoes and get a move on, Lindsey. Shades of John Edgar Hoover, I let you off your leash for a little romp and the next thing I know — '

'Mr. Richelieu. Sir. I'm on vacation. And it's nighttime. And this is my host's private telephone. How did — '

'Don't worry your little pointy head. I want you to hustle your buns over to the Golden Bear Inn in Berkeley — '

'Chief, I'm on vacation. And you know how I feel about Berkeley.' But that was a delaying tactic. Even as he spoke, Lindsey was crossing the living room, trotting upstairs to the guest bedroom, and extracting his pocket organizer and gold International Surety pencil from his woolen jacket.

' . . . name of Pierre Edmund Zipf, you got that? Body's still warm. Poor fellow was carrying an I.S. policyholder card. Apparently the bozo keeled over, they called 911, paramedics looked in his wallet and found the card and phoned us.'

Lindsey dropped the pocket organizer and gold pencil onto the bed and ran his free hand through his hair. 'Who's 'they,' Chief? And why did they call 911 and International Surety? Oh, never mind. Keeled over, hey? As in *unconscious?*'

'No, Lindsey. As in *deceased.*'

'Sounds like a routine claim. Why not just buck it down to Walnut Creek and let Elmer Mueller handle it? Isn't that what he's paid to do?'

'No, Lindsey. This one has SPUDS written all over it.'

Lindsey unconsciously reached for the cloissoné potato pin on his lapel. Anyone in International Surety knew that it meant he was a member of the Special Projects Unit/Detached Status, the company's elite corps of itinerant troubleshooters. Lindsey had worked his way up to the position of Deputy Director of SPUDS, but that didn't stop his boss, Desmond Richelieu, from phoning him from his aerie in Denver and sending him on a crackbrained errand.

'What's our interest?'

'This fellow Zipf was apparently engaged in a heated debate at the time of his death. He was the defendant in some kind of wacko trial.'

'In court?'

'You can call it that. The High Tribunal of the International Order of Loyal PEZ Aficionados. They were holding this cockamamie Star Chamber and Zipf was accused of something, apparently a forgery. And he was carrying on about ethics — '

'Did you say PEZ Aficionados? PEZ?'

'You getting deaf in your old age, Lindsey? Yes, PEZ.'

'As in *candy*?'

'Yes, as in candy. What's the matter with you? The air too thick down there at sea level?'

Lindsey lowered his weight onto the bed. 'Let me get this straight, Chief. This fellow Zipf was the defendant in a mock trial and he got overwrought, maybe the weight of his guilt was more than he could bear, and he dropped dead in the middle of the proceedings?'

'That's what it looks like. There was even a doctor on the spot and he took one look and said there was nothing he could do, Zipf was dead. *Kaput.* Thou wast not born for death, immortal Bird. But this bird was as dead as a dodo.'

'I still don't see what — '

'You're our ace collectibles man, Lindsey. Boot up your laptop and log onto KlameNet/ Plus and take a look at Zipf's policy. Somebody named Albicocco, Connie Albicocco, sounds like a sweetheart, phoned in the news to I.S. and I checked it out and it looks as if Zipf not only had a life policy, he had a personal property floater for his PEZ collection.'

Lindsey heard himself make an *ulp!* sound. 'Don't tell me, he had a valuable item in his pocket and he fell down and crushed it.'

'Worse,' Richelieu resumed. 'Miz Albicocco says she was the presiding officer at his

85

trial and depending on how the trial comes out, the collection might be junk or it might be worth a fortune.'

Lindsey groaned. He stood up and wandered out of the bedroom, onto the upstairs gallery of the Coffman house. The gallery was carpeted a deep golden-olive shade. There was a wrought-iron railing along its edge. The living room was below. Eric looked up at Lindsey, inquiringly. Lindsey shrugged.

'Where is this collection now?' he asked Richelieu. He still held Coffman's cordless phone to his ear. 'Is it damaged? Is there even a claim?'

'Lindsey.' The temperature on the gallery dropped forty degrees.

'Yes, Chief.'

'Lindsey, I want you to think very hard. I am directing you to handle this case. I *am* your Director, isn't that right? That's my title, Director of SPUDS, and you're Deputy Director of SPUDS. That means you work for me. I tell you what to do. I want you to go to this Golden Bear establishment and get ahold of this Miz Albicocco and find out what the blazes is happening out there and for once in your life earn your paycheck.'

Richelieu cut the connection before Lindsey could respond, and Lindsey knew better than to phone him back.

*   *   *

The Golden Bear Inn had been built in the 1920s, when Berkeley still called itself the Athens of the West and the favorite architectural conceit was a cross between California brown shingle and neo-Tudor. The building featured a stucco roof lovingly crafted to simulate thatch and half-timbered walls.

There was no yellow crime scene tape around the entrance to the Pine Room but there was a uniformed officer at the door and Lindsey had to show his International Surety ID to get past the officer. Her nametag read, *Nielson*.

Officer Nielson directed Lindsey to the sergeant in charge of the site. Lindsey introduced himself and handed over a business card. The sergeant took the card and handed Lindsey one of her own. He slipped it into his pocket. He'd already read the nametag on her uniform jacket. *Craigie*. Sergeant Craigie.

Pierre Edmund Zipf lay on a table on a low dais. A white linen cloth covered the table. There were microphones spaced along the table and chairs behind it. A couple of coroner's technicians were working on Mr. Zipf, and a police evidence technician was snapping photos.

A banner hung above the table, with words spelled out in giant simulated candy lozenges. WELCOME PEZ-HEADS.

A couple of dozen people were scattered around the room, talking quietly in clusters. Lindsey took a quick survey. Age ranged from preteens up after their bedtimes to a couple of relics who must be up past theirs. Not much ethnic diversity. More males than females.

A typical room full of collectors.

'Excuse, *señor*, but I recognize your *camote*, how you call, your potato, *sí*? You are from the *espuds*, no?'

Lindsey stared at the man. He couldn't have been more than 25 years old. He wore his black hair parted in the middle and slicked down with shiny oil, a pencil-thin jet-black mustache, a blue double-breasted suit with broad pointed lapels, a white-on-white shirt and a hand-painted tie with a picture of a Hawaiian dancing girl.

'Yes, I'm from SPUDS.'

'Eduardo Fonseca de Alarcón y Albénez.' The man clicked his heels and bowed. When he snapped erect Lindsey saw that he was wearing yellow shoes with needle-like tips and elevator heels, and even a pair of what looked like yellow kidskin gloves to match the shoes. He was doing the worst imitation of a young Cesar Romero Lindsey had ever seen.

'What can I do for you, Mr. — '

'Doctor. If you please. *Por favor*.'

'Yes.'

'I have the honor, sir, to represent the Affiliated PEZ Collectors of California, and I assume, sir, you have come here to, how you say, make the adjudgment? Adjudication? Of the authenticness, yes? Of the true *Rastreador Ricardo*.'

He clicked his heels and bowed again.

Lindsey had got as far as 'I don't know

what — ' when a young woman in blue jeans and an imprinted sweatshirt intervened.

'Mr. Lindsey?' She stuck her hand out and shook Lindsey's. She was wearing latex surgical gloves but pulled them off to shake hands. There was a picture of a giant PEZ dispenser on her sweatshirt. The sweatshirt had a two-handed pocket for keeping warm on chilly days. The giant PEZ dispenser had the head of a green-skinned, hook-nosed witch. 'I'm Connie Albicocco. I'm sorry about Eddie here.' She tilted her head toward Fonseca-and-so-forth.

Fonseca's complexion reddened and he said, 'This is intolerable. Utterly intolerable.'

'He likes to make a fuss. Run along, Eddie.'

'*Señorita*, you will hear from my, how you say, *abogado*, yes, in the *mañana*.' He made a half bow to Lindsey. '*Adiós, señor*.' He marched across the room and planted himself on a metal folding chair. He crossed his arms across his chest and stared straight ahead.

At the other side of the Pine Room a group of hobbyists were debating a point, waving their arms and occasionally raising their voices. Words popped out. 'Epoxy extrusion.' 'Slovenia.' 'Duckula.' 'Stem and head just didn't match.' 'Bubblepack.' 'Wretched shampoo cap.' 'Make-a-face.'

At 'make-a-face,' there was a hush, as if a sacred name had been uttered, but quickly the debate resumed.

Connie Albicocco was still standing in front of Lindsey. She wore her honey-colored hair in a ponytail. She was slim and she kept working her fingers in and out, in and out.

'Miss Albicocco,' Lindsey said, 'I still don't understand why you phoned International Surety. It's tragic that Mr. Zipf has died.' He put on his polite condolence face. 'But why couldn't his heirs file a death claim in the normal manner?'

'It's the Dick Tracy,' she said.

'The Dick Tracy.'

'Yes. What Dr. Fonseca calls *El Rastreador*.'

Lindsey blinked. 'Is he actually a doctor? A *medical* doctor?'

'So he claims.' Connie smiled nervously. 'He joined the Order via our Web page. He claims to represent this splinter group, these so-called Affiliated Collectors who, as far as I can find out, consist of him all by his lonesome. Fonseca — the whole bit — is his screen name. I don't know his real name.'

'Okay, okay. This is moving a little too fast for me. What's this about *El Rastreador* and Dick Tracy?'

'He had a Dick Tracy PEZ dispenser. Really very nice. The yellow fedora, the pointed nose and chin.'

'You mean the comic strip character. Not Ralph Byrd or Warren Beatty.'

'Who?' She tilted her head.

'Never mind. The comic strip, yes?'

'That's right. But Mister PEZ there — '

'I thought his name was Zipf.'

'That's right. Pierre Edmund Zipf. His initials spell out PEZ. He always said that's what got him interested in collecting PEZ. He called himself Mister PEZ and he started a mail-order business.

Mister PEZ's Pezzeria.' When Lindsey looked puzzled she said, 'Like, pizzeria? It's a play on words. Pezzeria.'

'Got it. Right.'

She sighed and stopped twisting her fingers. Apparently she felt she'd accomplished something important, making Lindsey understand about Mr. PEZ's Pezzeria and the Dick Tracy PEZ dispenser. Unfortunately, he didn't understand at all.

'Why did you call International Surety? Why was it important to get me out here?'

'Because of the Tribunal.'

Lindsey nodded. This wasn't the first time in his career that he'd felt like Alice down the rabbit hole.

'The Tribunal,' he repeated.

The evidence technician had finished taking photographs and the coroner's squad were sliding Mister PEZ's body off the speaker's table and onto a gurney. Lindsey got a look at the face before the coroner's techs covered it. It was impossible to tell whether Zipf had been as pallid in life as he was in death, as fleshy and as pasty looking.

Then the gurney was gone.

Under Sgt. Craigie's watchful eye, Officer Nielson was taking the names and addresses of all the PEZ collectors in the Pine Room and sending them home. When Dr. Fonseca's turn arrived, Sgt. Craigie asked him to stay behind.

Craigie called Connie Albicocco and Hobart Lindsey over. 'I want to get to the bottom of this before we close up shop and go home.'

'Bottom of what?' Fonseca's accent seemed to come and go like a cloud on a summer's afternoon.

'The death of Mr. Zipf.'

'He suffered a cerebral embolism. What you laymen call a stroke.'

'That's your diagnosis, Doctor?'

'I examined the man. There's no question.'

'Well, we'll see what the coroner has to say. Now suppose you folks tell me what was going on here. Looks like a collectors' swap-meet.' She pointed to the banner above the speakers' table. 'Or was it some kind of trial? Miss — ' she consulted a pad ' — Albicocco?'

Connie Albicocco shot a withering look at Eduardo Fonseca. 'Mister PEZ — Pierre Zipf — had a Dick Tracy PEZ dispenser.'

Sgt. Craigie grinned. 'I used to collect PEZ dispensers. I must have had twenty. My favorite was Bugs Bunny.' She stopped and removed the grin from her face. 'What about it?'

'There never was a Dick Tracy PEZ dispenser. It's a fake.'

'What do you mean? Either it's a PEZ dispenser or it isn't, hey? You put the little candies in and . . . ' She gestured. 'Right?'

'Hah!' Fonseca laughed. 'Forgive me, Sergeant, but your ignorance is in the extremity.'

Connie Albicocco said, 'There have been lots of phony PEZ dispensers over the years. Hopalong Cassidy, Pee Wee Herman, Leonard Nimoy with Spock ears. There was even a fake Hitler PEZ dispenser. They look real, they even work with the PEZ candies, but they were never issued by the company that owns PEZ and they're not legitimate PEZ collectibles.'

'And you're challenging the Dick Tracy?' Lindsey put in.

'It was a falsity, *absolutamente*,' Fonseca asserted.

'But Mr. Zipf claimed it was real?' Craigie asked.

Albicocco and Fonseca nodded assent.

'And what difference would that make?'

'Zipf claimed he had a whole Tracy series. Tess Trueheart, Frank Redrum, Flattop, Gravel Gertie. If they're legitimate, they're apparently unique copies, maybe test pressings for a line that was never issued, they're worth thousands of dollars. If they're fakes — any clever collector who knows how to work in plastic, even has a friend in art school or a workshop — you can fake the Tracy's and they're just a clever novelty, hardly worth anything.'

Lindsey cleared his throat. 'I don't know much about PEZ, but I've worked with a lot of collectibles. Why don't you just contact the company?'

Once more Albicocco and Fonseca agreed on something. 'No way,' Fonseca said. 'The company is in *Alemania*, how you say, in Germany, but collectors try many times to find out and they say, their records not to show nothing. They give to *licensadores*, how you to saying it, licensees in different countries. Hong Kong, Hungary, Nueva Jersey, Japan, Mexico, España. To find out all PEZ *productos — aii, no es posíble!*'

'That right?' queried Sgt. Craigie.

'I'm afraid it's right,' Connie Albicocco confirmed.

Sgt. Craigie shook her head. 'I guess we'll all just have to go home and wait for the autopsy report.'

Albicocco and Fonseca started for the exit.

Lindsey jumped ahead and spread his arms across the doorway. 'Wait a minute!'

They halted.

'Where is this alleged Dick Tracy PEZ dispenser?'

Fonseca shrugged.

Albicocco turned and looked back toward the speakers' table where the ill-fated Tribunal had assembled.

'International Surety issued a floater policy to Mr. Zipf. We may be out a lot of money if that little toy is lost. I suggest we stay here and search this room, and nobody leave until we find it.'

'Damn, Mr. Lindsey.' Craigie grimaced. 'There must have been twenty people here earlier. You should have spoken up right away. Anyone could have carried that thing away.'

Lindsey ran his hand across his eyes. 'You're right.' He paused. 'Still,' he resumed, 'let's give it a try. If nobody minds.'

Craigie looked at the others. 'Up to you,' she said.

Connie Albicocco said, 'Okay by me. Let's hunt.'

Lindsey said, 'And if you don't mind — maybe we could all turn our pockets out.' He shrugged diffidently as he made the suggestion, and started with his own pockets. A wallet, a comb, a set of keys . . .

Dr. Fonseca made a sudden break for the hallway, but Lindsey was in his path and blocked him. As they struggled, Sgt. Craigie grabbed Fonseca from behind and pulled him off Lindsey.

Fonseca stood panting and glaring

from Lindsey to Craigie to Albicocco. 'All right,' he barked in unaccented English. 'I picked it up when Zipf fell over.' He reached into his impeccably tailored suit pocket with one yellow-kid-gloved hand and removed a little plastic candy dispenser.

'Here,' he said, 'You might as well have the damned thing.' He tossed the toy at Connie Albicocco.

Albicocco jumped back and Dick Tracy clattered to the floor.

Lindsey looked at Albicocco, then at Fonseca, then once more at Albicocco.

Sgt. Craigie said, 'How peculiar. Would you hand me that thing, Miss Albicocco?'

The young woman backed away from the toy. 'No,' she said.

'Why not?'

'I won't touch it. It's death to touch it. It killed Pierre Zipf and it should have killed you, Fonseca. I don't know why it didn't.'

Sgt. Craigie held up her hand. 'Wait a minute, everybody. I don't know what's happening here, but before anyone says another word I'm going to read you all your Miranda rights.' She turned and said, 'Officer Nielson, you're witness to this.'

'Right, Sergeant.'

Once Craigie had slipped her Miranda card back into her pocket she looked at Connie Albicocco once more. 'Are you sure you don't want to pick that toy up, Miss?'

'I won't touch it!'

Fonseca bent and lifted the toy. He held it in front of him and looked at it. Lindsey could see the lovingly-made and painted features on Dick Tracy's face.

'Officer Nielson here has some evidence baggies. You just drop that in carefully, Dr. Fonseca. Nobody else touch Dick Tracy.' To Connie Albicocco, Craigie said, 'You want to tell me why Dr. Fonseca should be dead, Miss Albicocco?'

'It's the nicotine. It was all over the PEZ dispenser. I had custody during the Tribunal. I was so careful. I smeared it on and I didn't get a drop on myself, and when Pierre picked it up to show the Tribunal it just went through his skin the way it was supposed to and he dropped dead.'

'Dropped dead, did he?' Craigie asked. 'And then what?'

'And then — then I saw you steal it, damn you, Fonseca! Why didn't you die?'

Fonseca looked at the bag Officer Nielson was holding. She had sealed it carefully and was laboriously filling out an evidence slip to go with it.

'My gloves, I guess.' Fonseca shrugged.

'But nicotine should go right through kidskin. Through any kind of leather.'

Fonseca grinned sheepishly. Lindsey thought he might actually be blushing. '*Desculpamé por favor, señorita.* I have not so much the *dinero, sí?* The, how you say, dollars. *Mis guantes*, my how you say, gloves, they are only the *imitaciónes baratos*, the imitations cheaps. They are made of the rubber to look like the leather.'

'I think they saved your life,' Sgt. Craigie commented. 'And where is the rest of that nicotine now, Miss Albicocco?'

Connie Albicocco slipped a hand inside the double pocket of her PEZ dispenser sweatshirt and brought it back out holding a tiny vial of clear liquid. It could have been a crack container, but this was a different kind of poison.

'I might as well use it on myself,' she sobbed.

But before she could unscrew the black plastic cap Officer Nielson knocked the vial from her hand. It landed without breaking and Nielson babied it gently into another evidence bag. She pulled her pen from her pocket and started filling out a second evidence slip.

Sgt. Craigie clipped a pair of handcuffs onto Connie Albicocco's wrists. 'You'll have to come with me, Miss. I'm sorry, I have to tell you you're in very big trouble. Very, very big trouble.'

Albicocco sprang at Fonseca but her cuffed wrists impaired her and Officer Nielson subdued her easily. 'You pig,' she spat at Fonseca. 'Everything was working perfectly until you tried to stab me in the back! How could you — ' She halted, panting.

Fonseca smiled sheepishly.

'What did you do?' Craigie responded.

'Well, I did steal Dick Tracy there. For a while.'

Craigie laughed. 'A forty-nine cent toy? I don't think anybody is going to be too concerned.'

'Oh, no?' Albicocco snarled. 'Ask him where I *got* the nicotine. *He's* the chemist. *He's* the one who knew how to refine it from a couple of packs of cigarettes.'

'Is this true?' Craigie asked.

'I had to have the Dick Tracy. I don't care about money. It was the only one in the world and I had to have it. You don't understand.' Fonseca stood with head bowed, staring at the pointed tips of his yellow shoes.

'I do understand,' Lindsey said. 'I understand a lot about collecting and I understand you, Dr. Fonseca.'

Craigie addressed Lindsey. 'And you, sir — I know you got here after the crime took place, but if you don't mind giving us your statement as well . . . '

Lindsey said, 'No, I don't mind. Just so long as I can get back to my friends' house and modem in my report afterwards.'

★　★　★

103

Blue skies, white fluffy clouds and a bright, early-morning sun. Lindsey pulled the borrowed station wagon into the Coffmans' driveway and dragged himself into the house. Unshaven, rumpled and stale, he still responded to the cooking odors and gratefully joined the family for breakfast.

Between sips of coffee and bites of pancake, he told the night's story. When he finished, Miriam commented, 'So this Fonseca was a real doctor after all.'

'Yes, but not an MD. He was a chemist. He prepared the concentrated nicotine just as Connie Albicocco said he did. What a guy — straight-arrow type, wife and kiddies, the works. He only dressed like a gigolo and slathered grease on his hair and used that phony accent when he was out in the collecting world. And of course his name wasn't Fonseca.'

The two Coffman girls sat with rapt expressions on their faces. Telling their schoolmates about this was going to be *so cool!*

Eric Coffman shook his head. 'You've told me that collectors are strange people,

Bart, but this takes the cake. Albicocco wore latex gloves so she wouldn't contaminate the evidence, did she?'

'She said.'

'And she and Fonseca were in cahoots all along — until they'd eliminated Zipf — and then there was the famous falling out among thieves.' He sliced into a stack of pancakes and conveyed a golden morsel to his mouth.

'Eric.' Lindsey winked at his host. 'When Albicocco and Fonseca go to trial, if they ask you to represent them, what will you tell them?'

Before Coffman would reply his wife said, 'Eric doesn't do criminal, Bart. You know that. Here, let me top off your coffee.'

4

Chinese Gunboats

Sometimes Marvia Plum enjoyed the job of watch commander and sometimes she found it boring and irritating. Then she longed for the days when she was a patrol cop, dealing with different situations at a moment's notice. Robbery in progress, domestic violence call, drug deal going down, or just a barking dog complaint.

Then she'd made sergeant and transferred to Homicide and spent her time tracking down killers. Talk about your rush — there was nothing like closing a murder case, confronting a suspect and knowing that you'd collared a serious bad guy and booked him into City Jail. But now she was sitting at a desk and it was almost three in the morning and by this time of night there was seldom much action in Berkeley.

That's when the yowl came down from

Emergency Dispatch. The night manager at the All-Star Gym on Barbara Jordan Boulevard had punched nine-one-one and started hollering at the dispatcher. Somebody was dead and the manager said it was murder. No need to send an emergency medical team. The manager was a former airborne ranger and he knew that a man who'd taken a large-caliber bullet through the forehead, who had an exit wound the size of an orange in the back of his cranium, whose brains were scattered all over the hot white tile wall of the steam room, and whose heart had already stopped pumping blood down the steam-room drain, was definitely and irreversibly dead.

The All-Star Gym didn't need medics, it needed cops.

★   ★   ★

There was a cruiser in front of the All-Star Gym, its light-bar flashing, when Marvia pulled her unit to the curb. She trotted to the glass front doors. Jeff Felton, a veteran patrol officer, opened one door for her and locked it behind her. There was a sign posted, *Temporarily Closed*. The All-Star Gym advertised its twenty-four hour operation but anyone who arrived for a pre-dawn workout this morning would be disappointed.

Felton briefed Marvia on the situation as they crossed the lobby. The building's lights were blazing but their voices echoed in the nearly empty, normally-bustling lobby. There were just nine people in the building when the killing occurred. George Carman, the night manager, had been manning the front desk. Carman's younger brother, Timmy, had just entered the men's steam room on his nightly rounds, and found Mort Greller, a regular at the All-Star, sweating out a chill. The others were scattered through the gym's sparsely occupied facilities.

Now George Carman emerged from behind the desk and greeted Marvia. She worked out at the All-Star Gym herself; it was a favorite hangout for off-duty cops, staffers from radio station KRED (just up the block on Barbara Jordan Boulevard), and off-duty workers from local businesses.

'Timmy's really upset, Sergeant.' Carman didn't look too robust himself, Marvia thought. 'He was in there, I think he wanted Mr. Greller to finish up so he could swab the place out, he does that every night. Somebody must have come in right behind him, walked up to Greller and shot him pointblank. Then he just calmly walked out again. Timmy's not handling it too well.'

Marvia nodded understandingly. She knew Timmy Carman; most of Berkeley did. Timmy was a gentle soul, semi-autistic, with definite qualities of the savant. It was hard to know what went on inside his head, hard to carry on a conversation with him. He lived with his older brother, and George was devoted to Timmy.

'Where was everybody else when this happened?' Marvia asked, 'and where are they now?'

Felton told her. Some had been in the weight room pumping iron, others in the cardiovascular center, and one or two in the swimming pool. They were assembled now in a small room usually reserved for staff meetings.

'Officer Nardiello is babysitting. He's making them write out statements of when they arrived at the gym and everything they've done since they got here.'

'We can verify arrivals,' George Carman put in. 'They all run their membership cards through the turnstile when they arrive. The computer logs everybody in.'

Marvia liked that. 'How about when they leave, I don't recall a card-reader on the way out when I've been here.'

'There's a counter on the turnstile. We know how many people have left, but not who or when.'

That wasn't so good. Carman could tell her who had entered the gym today, and how many members had left. But if the numbers didn't jibe, he could not tell her who was lurking somewhere in the building. Alternately, somebody could have entered the gym much earlier in the day and just hung around, then committed the crime and hustled out unnoticed.

'All right. You said Timmy's not taking it so well. Let's go talk to him, do you think he's up to that?'

George Carman considered. 'He knows

you, Sergeant. He knows there's been a crime — I think he does, anyhow — so it might help him to talk to you. Come on, then.' He led the way around the counter, into the little store where gym supplies were displayed in glass counters. There were sweats and tees and tights, expensive gym shoes of half a dozen brands, water bottles and gym bags and wristbands and leather gloves designed to keep the rough canvas of the heavy punching bag from scraping the knuckles of boxers in training. There were a variety of novelties that people could put on display in their homes or offices that would say to visitors, *I'm modern, I'm up to date, I take care of my body, I work out at the gym, I'm going to live forever.*

Wrong.

Timmy Carman sat in a padded chair used for trying on gym shoes. He was staring at an All-Star Gym souvenir snowglobe. He sat motionless as long as the flakes swirled and danced. When they had all reached the bottom of the globe he turned it upside down, waited until they'd risen — or fallen — and then set it

111

on its base once more.

Marvia said, 'Timmy, do you know me?'

He ignored her.

She took the snowglobe gently from him and put it on a counter. She said, 'I'm Sergeant Plum, Timmy, remember me?'

He looked at her face and smiled. He said, something that sounded like, *Chinese gunboats*.

Marvia looked at George Carman, who shrugged, then back at Timmy. 'Gunboats?' she asked. 'As in naval warfare?'

Gunboats, he repeated, or maybe the word was *gumbo*.

'Chinese gumbo?' Marvia asked. 'Chinese vegetable stew?'

Timmy started bouncing in his chair. He said *no* over and over. Marvia said, 'What, Timmy? Didn't I understand you?'

'Gunboats. Chinese gunboats. Gunboats. Gunboats.'

Marvia inhaled deeply, noticing the faint odor of liniment and perspiration that pervaded the place. 'Chinese gunboats,' she repeated.

Timmy held his hands in front of his

face, the thumbs and forefingers connected to make a rough square. He said, 'There are ninety two thousand, one hundred sixty squares in the steam room. Fifteen thousand, three hundred sixty big ones, seventy-six thousand, eight hundred little ones. That makes ninety two thousand, one hundred sixty.'

He grinned beatifically.

'George, do you know what he's talking about?'

George Carman held his hands out helplessly. 'I'm sorry.'

'Timmy,' Marvia said, 'do you know what happened in the steam room? Can you tell us what you saw?'

Timmy tilted his head and looked straight at Marvia. He liked her. She was one of the few people other than George he would talk to. Anyone else, including employees and regular customers at the gym, he avoided. He would work around them. When they spoke to him he would turn his face away and ignore them.

'Lots of squares.' Timmy nodded. 'Chinese gunboats.' He nodded to himself, a faraway look in his eyes. 'Two hundred thirty-one

Chinese gunboats.'

To George Carman, Marvia said, 'Do you think he could handle going back there? Would he freak out if we took him back?'

'I think he'd be okay. I'll stay with him, I'll hold his hand.'

They descended the short flight of terra cotta stairs to the basement. The men's and women's locker rooms were there, steam rooms, saunas, showers, and pool. Jeff Felton accompanied them, his police uniform incongruous as they passed posters of grimly grinning athletes in tights or sweats.

At Felton's direction, George Carman had shut off the steam and locked the heavy glass door to the men's steam room. Felton had strung yellow crime scene tape across the doorway for good measure.

Through the glass Marvia could see Mort Greller. It wasn't difficult to trace the trajectory of his body. He must have been sitting on the upper ledge, his back to the wall, when he was shot. A large-caliber round to the face, exiting through the anterior cranium. The spatter on the wall had run, due to the hot steam that had filled the room. A square white tile was smashed and blackened; Marvia expected that the distorted remnant of the bullet would be found in the plaster behind it.

Instantaneously dead, the back of his head smashing against the wall, Greller had bounced forward, tumbling off the ledge, to land face-down near the drain in the middle of the floor.

'What did you see, Timmy?'

Now a series of expressions pursued one another across Timmy Carman's face. 'Only ninety-two thousand one hundred fifty nine now. Have to put in a new one. Fix it up. Fix the tile, George, I'll fix the tile.'

His lips pursed, George Carman said, 'We'll get it, Timmy. Don't worry about it.' He turned toward Marvia. 'He loves to count things. He's a math whiz, you know.'

Frowning, Marvia asked what the numbers meant.

'I'm not certain,' George Carman

replied. 'I think he was counting the tiles in the steam room. What did he say — '

'Fifteen thousand three hundred sixty big, seventy-six thousand eight hundred little,' Timmy interjected. He pointed through the glass, moving his fingertip in tiny increments, like a conductor leading a symphony of Lilliputians.

'He counted every single tile in that room?' Marvia exclaimed.

'It's hard to tell. More likely he counted the number of rows and columns and worked it out in his mind. He loves math problems. Sometimes he'll stand in the office and our office manager will run computer problems while Timmy stands by and solves them faster than our Circuitron. He's pretty amazing. Never wrong, either.'

'And the other numbers? The huge numbers he was spouting? Timmy, what were the other numbers?'

He looked like a smart, loyal dog who'd been asked to perform a trick that he had totally mastered and was proud to demonstrate. 'Fifteen thousand three hundred sixty plus seventy six thousand eight hundred makes ninety two thousand one hundred sixty squared is eight billion four hundred ninety three million four hundred sixty five thousand six hundred. Square root of nine-two-one-six-oh is three-oh-three-point-five-seven-eight-six- five-five-three-seven-six-two.'

Marvia exchanged glances with George Carman, exhaled and shook her head. 'Can you tell me what happened in the steam room, Timmy? What happened to Mr. Greller?'

Timmy waved his hands in front of his face. 'Too much steam. Couldn't see. Just Chinese gunboats.'

'Okay. You were cleaning, is that right?'

'Cleaning. All the squares.'

'And then what happened? Mr. Greller was having a steam bath and someone came in?'

'Someone. White, very white. *Mmmm.* Shot Mr. Greller. *BOOM!* And went out.'

'Man or woman?'

Timmy didn't respond.

'Did the person say anything?'

No reaction. Timmy was staring at the body. The crime scene wagon would be here any minute, and the evidence tech's would start measuring and photographing and collecting materials. They'd get the bullet, what was left of it. Then the coroner's squad would arrive. They had to come all the way from Fourth Street in Oakland, it would take them a while.

Timmy pressed his nose against the glass door and stared at the remains of Mort Greller. He began to cry. His brother caught a nod from Marvia and led him away from the grisly sight. Timmy said, 'Thirty-seven-point-five French gunboats. Nine English gunboats. Two hundred thirty-one Chinese gunboats.'

George Carman said, 'It's okay, Timmy. Let's go get a glass of apple juice.'

Timmy said, 'Two hundred thirty-one Chinese gunboats squared is fifty three thousand three hundred sixty-one Chinese Chinese gunboats gunboats.' He grinned at his brother.

Marvia addressed Officer Felton. 'What do you think, Jeff? Ever see anything like this?'

Felton scratched his short-trimmed thatch of salt-and-pepper hair. 'You got an eye witness to the killing, couple of feet from the shooter, and he couldn't see anything because of the steam and besides that he's an autistic savant. Definitely one for the books.'

'Keep an eye on the brothers, Jeff. I'm going to see how Nardiello's doing with the rest of the exercise mavens.' She turned away, then turned back. 'George, do you think Timmy could answer some questions for me at the women's steam room? It's just the same as the men's, maybe he could show me what happened.'

George Carman said, 'He could probably handle that a lot better than the men's.'

★ ★ ★

Marvia made her way to the meeting room.

Officer Nardiello presided over the half-dozen men and women like a grad student proctoring a freshman final. Marvia entered the room and stood quietly in the rear. The six civilians were seated around a conference table while Nardiello stood at a rostrum.

Nardiello had scouted up half a dozen lined pads, presumably courtesy of All-Star Gym, and the civilians were busily writing with stubby yellow pencils. Official forms would follow later, in all likelihood, but this was a way to get a quick report from everyone involved . . . or everyone who might be involved.

And like a good proctor, Nardiello permitted no talking or passing of notes during the exam.

Soon Nardiello collected the reports. He handed them to Marvia. She compared them to the list of late arrivals at the gym provided by George Carman. They checked out. The names were Jem Waller, Jessie Loman, Phyllis di Biasi, Shaughnessy, Millicent Raines, and Yaeko Kato. In addition to Mort Greller, of course. Shaughnessy seemed to have no first name.

One of the civilians, a woman in a dazzling set of Cal Tech sweats and fancy gym shoes, stood up and turned to Marvia. 'Sergeant Plum,' she said, 'Phyllis di Biasi, KRED. Remember me?'

Marvia had recently worked a messy case at the nearby radio station and had questioned di Biasi more than once. '*Techno News Update*, wasn't it?'

'That's right.' The woman grinned. She had olive colored skin and glossy, thick hair as black as midnight. She extended her hand and Marvia shook it. 'Do you know how long this is going on?' di Biasi asked. 'I'd like to finish my workout and get home and to bed.'

'Sorry about that. We'll have you out of here as soon as possible.'

'And how soon is that?'

'As soon as possible.' Under her breath, Marvia counted to five. 'Someone was murdered in this building. I'm sure you know that. This is not a simple matter.'

Di Biasi stood with her hands on her hips, then reluctantly returned to her seat.

Marvia riffled the brief statements until she came to di Biasi's. The woman claimed she had done a late broadcast at KRED and come to the gym from the studio with Jem Waller and Jessie Loman. Waller was chief engineer at the station

121

and Loman was a producer. They'd left the station and walked the short distance on Barbara Jordan Boulevard together.

There wasn't much problem with the time of the murder. The crash of the single shot, loud as it must have been and even though it echoed off the tile walls of the steam room, would have been muffled by the thick walls, heavy glass door, and loud hissing of the steam. But Timmy Carman, as nearly as his brother could deduce, had run from the room just seconds after the killer's departure and raced to tell George what had happened.

Marvia leafed through the other statements. Waller's and Loman's corroborated di Biasi's. At the time of death, they indicated, Waller and Loman had been in the strength room working on their muscle groups. Di Biasi was next door, lifting free weights.

Shaughnessy 'Himself,' as the man so coyly put it, had come from his bar and grille, around the corner from BJB on Huntington Way. Millicent Raines worked at Shaughnessy's. She'd helped close up and had accompanied her boss to the gym. They'd been riding stationary bikes in the cardiovascular center when Greller was shot.

And the last customer was Yaeko Kato, the tall UC grad student and part-time waitress at the Bara Miyako restaurant on Barbara Jordan Boulevard. She'd helped the owners, her uncle and aunt, to close up. Then she'd escorted the blind chef, her grandfather, to his little apartment nearby. Then she'd come to the gym to swim laps. Her wet hair was still wrapped in a towel.

Marvia walked to the rostrum and stood beside Vince Nardiello. 'I'm sorry to inconvenience you all, but you understand the need. You'll just have to be patient a little longer. Unless somebody wants to confess right now, and let the rest of us go home.'

The joke landed with a dull thud.

'Okay,' Marvia resumed. 'Did anyone here know Mort Greller?'

Shaughnessy 'Himself' and Millicent Raines both raised their hands. 'Himself' said, 'Milly waited on Mort all the time.'

'That so? Let's step out in the hallway for a moment.'

In response to Marvia's question, Milly stated that Greller had stopped into Shaughnessy's just a couple of hours ago. He'd been in an expansive mood, the bar had been quiet tonight, and he'd gone out of his way to chat her up.

'Do you know what he was so happy about?' Marvia asked.

'He was just back from a business trip. He's going to manufacture CD-ROMs and circuit chips in China. He'd just been on KRED, on di Biasi's show. He said she was steamed. She used to work for his company. She claimed he'd stolen her best ideas and was making a fortune and she was barely scraping a living. I asked him why he'd go on her show after that, and he said he liked to rub it in. He knew she'd try and get him to admit what he'd done, on the air, and then she could sue him because they record all their programs, but he was too smart to fall for that. He was chuckling all over the place. He was a slimy bastard and I'm glad he's dead.'

Marvia gave her a look.

Millicent Raines inhaled sharply. 'That

doesn't mean I killed him. I didn't do it.'

Marvia said, 'No, it doesn't. Okay, please retake your seat. I'll be back in a few minutes.'

Shaughnessy backed up Raines's statement but he had little to add. He'd been behind the mahogany all night serving up beverages and the occasional sandwich. He ran a friendly neighborhood bar, he knew his customers and he spent many an hour trading risqué stories with regulars.

He'd seen Greller talking with Raines but Greller had sat at a table, not at the bar, and Shaughnessy hadn't overheard their conversation.

After Shaughnessy and Raines re-entered the conference room, Marvia rejoined Jeff Felton and the Carman brothers in the gym store upstairs. Within minutes they had descended again, this time to the women's steam room. George Carman turned off the steam and shortly the air in the room was clear.

Marvia stepped inside. The white tile walls radiated heavy, damp heat. She said, 'Timmy, could you show us what happened?'

Timmy Carman went through more of his personal mathematical mantra until Marvia asked him again to show her what had happened.

'No,' he shook his head, 'the men's. This is the ladies'.'

Marvia nodded. 'That's right, Timmy, but could you make believe this is the men's steam room? Make believe . . . pretend?'

He grinned impishly. 'Improvisational theater, simulated steam room, *Who Killed Mort Greller*, scene one, take two, action!'

Marvia looked at George Carman. She couldn't read his expression.

'All right, Timmy. Officer Felton will play Mr. Greller, you be yourself, I'll be the other person. Is that good?'

'Good.'

Felton let Timmy position him on the upper ledge, his back against the wall. The walls were covered with white tiles, three inches square. The ledges and the floor were covered with smaller tiles. That would account for Timmy's math. The walls and ledges were still dripping with condensed steam. Felton's uniform would be soaked. All in the line of duty.

Timmy crouched at the end of the seating ledge. He scrubbed the tiles with an invisible brush, working imaginary disinfectant into the porcelain and grout.

With George Carman holding the door open, Marvia strode toward Felton. She raised her hand, simulating a weapon with the old child's gesture of curled fingers, pointed forefinger, upraised thumb. She extended her arm toward Felton.

Timmy said, 'No, closer.'

She took a step.

'Closer. Point eight-nine-four meters.'

'How could you tell?' she asked.

'Easy,' Timmy replied. 'Easy. Easy.' He offered no more explanation than that.

But Marvia persisted. 'You said there was too much steam to see, Timmy. How could you measure the distance from the weapon to the victim?'

Timmy made a strange sound, *Yi-yi-yi*. He flailed his arms as if to clear away obscuring clouds of steam. 'Flash!' he exclaimed. 'Smash!'

Marvia shook her head. 'I don't

understand, Timmy. Help me, please.'

He stationed himself between Marvia and Felton. He pressed the palm of one hand against Marvia's fingertip, the muzzle of the simulated murder weapon. 'Flash!' He pressed his other palm against Felton's forehead. 'Smash!' He grinned happily, swinging his face from Marvia to Felton and back, chanting 'Flash! Smash! Flash! Smash!'

His brother took Timmy's two hands in his own and pressed them gently down. 'That's enough, Timmy, that's okay, isn't it, Sergeant Plum?'

Marvia said, 'That's just fine. Thank you, Timmy.' He smiled and backed away, then went back to scrubbing tile with his imaginary brush.

Marvia stood within arm's reach of Felton. Could Timmy really have measured the distance with that degree of precision, just by eye? An astonishing ability. She put it out of her mind for the moment, dropped her thumb against her forefinger and said, 'Bang!'

Timmy scuttled toward her and crouched at her feet.

As Felton pitched forward off the ledge, catching himself so he wouldn't crash face-first onto the tile floor, Marvia leaped back to avoid being knocked over.

Timmy grabbed her shoe. As she tugged away from him, controlled by unthinking reflex, he emitted two words in a voice that made Marvia's skin crawl. It sounded like a cross between a scream and a yodel. Timmy was saying, 'Chinese gunboats.'

* * *

At Marvia's suggestion, George Carman took his brother to the gym's little canteen for a snack and a glass of juice. Marvia and Officer Felton repaired to the gym store while Nardiello continued to ride herd on six restless exercise fanatics.

'Now I know what *Chinese gunboats* means,' Marvia said. 'Did you catch on, Jeff? Down in the steam room? And, by the way, I'm sorry about your uniform. You know department policy, so don't worry about it.'

Felton had a rueful expression on his

face. 'Sure I caught on. When that poor guy grabbed your foot. I guess you have to be old enough to have gray hair to remember when they called shoes gunboats. You think the killer has big feet?'

'Probably not that easy. Funny that Timmy would use an old expression like that, but he's a strange guy. Not stupid, autistics aren't stupid. They're just very strange people.'

Marvia stood with her back to Felton, studying the expensive gym shoes in a display case. At today's prices a cop could spend a month's pay on one gym outfit. The fanciest shoes in the case were marked with a size-and-nation-of-origin tag. The shoes were made in China. Three sizes were shown, based on US, European, and Asian scales. Eleven and a half, forty-six, two hundred ninety-five. *Fabrique en Chine.*

'Timmy said two hundred thirty-one Chinese gunboats. The killer was wearing Chinese gym shoes, size 231. That's 231, Asian shoe size!'

★ ★ ★

Marvia had to threaten to get a search warrant to measure Phyllis di Biasi's gym shoes. The threat, plus the fact that the size was recorded in the computerized sales records of the All-Star Gym, did the trick.

While Jem Waller and Jessie Loman were using the strength machines together, di Biasi was supposedly next door making like a female Arnold Schwarzenegger. She could have walked downstairs with a gun wrapped in a towel. Her light-colored sweats accounted for Timmy's description of the killer as 'white,' despite di Biasi's olive skin color.

Di Biasi had shot Mort Greller point-blank, Timmy Carman's statement proved that. She must have been shocked to realize that Timmy had witnessed the murder, but she was a cool enough character to know that he couldn't identify her in the billowing vapor of the steam room, and his autism would make it unlikely that he could tell the police anything at all.

Where was the murder weapon? It had to be somewhere in the building, and a thorough search would turn it up. A paraffin test on di Biasi was unlikely to succeed, but if di Biasi was wearing gloves when she fired the fatal shot, there would be residue on the outside of the gloves and there would probably be perspiration with recoverable DNA inside.

At least she hadn't shot the innocent Timmy. And she had a reason for killing Greller. The DA would surely go for first degree. She had premeditated, she had long-standing motive, and she brought the gun with her to the gym and disposed of it afterwards.

Hours later the shift changed at Berkeley police headquarters. Leaving the building in mufti, Marvia invited Felton and Nardiello out for a cup of coffee at Shaughnessy's, of all places. 'Himself' might be exhausted from the previous day's work and the night's excitement, but he wasn't too tired to supervise his employees as they opened the establishment for a new day's business.

Even at this hour, Shaughnessy's didn't lack for customers. There were the faithful who stopped in daily to breakfast off Shaughnessy's grille, there were a handful of dedicated drinkers who had to have an eye-opener to get their bleary days off to an alcoholic start, and there were a few celebrants who couldn't head for home without a nightcap even if the sun was up and the commuters were filling the street outside.

'A good night's work, men.' Marvia looked at Felton and at Nardiello. 'Hey, I'll not only buy the java, I'll spring for breakfast if anybody's hungry.'

While they waited for their food to arrive, Nardiello speculated on Phyllis di Biasi's fate. 'I can't blame her for offing that creep. I mean, I've heard of swiping other people's work, but rubbing her nose in it that way, that's too much.'

Jeff Felton laughed. 'Hey, Vince, what year is it, 1940? Come on, buddy.'

Nardiello frowned. 'What do you mean? Never mind, here's the food.'

Shaughnessy 'Himself' laid the dishes in front of them. Marvia extended a bill. Shaughnessy said, 'It's on the house, Sergeant.'

She shook her head. 'No can do, Shaughnessy. You know the rules.'

'Okay.' Shaughnessy shrugged, wrote out a check and dropped it on the table. Marvia picked it up and read the amount. She chuckled. Based on these prices, maybe it really was 1940.

Jeff Felton said, 'Di Biasi's lawyers will claim some chronic stress syndrome plus a triggering trauma. They'll probably play up Greller's rotten treatment of di Biasi. Then they'll claim emotional abuse going back to di Biasi's days working for Greller. And Greller's gloating to Millicent Raines after the show on KRED — that's perfect. Di Biasi's lawyers will play the KRED tape in the courtroom. Greller didn't just steal her work, he came back from China and poured salt in her wounds until the poor girl finally snapped.'

Nardiello took a big mouthful of fried egg and washed it down with a healthy swig of orange juice. 'You think she'll get off?'

Felton turned to Marvia. 'What do you say, Sarge? What's going to happen to poor little Miz di Biasi?'

Marvia smiled a peculiar smile. She said, 'I think she'll be on the street again

134

before you can say *Chinese gunboats*. She'll probably get her job back at KRED.' She thought for a moment, contemplating a morsel of toasted muffin. 'I expect she'll sue Greller's heirs for the money they make off her invention, and then she'll probably run for mayor of Berkeley.'

Shaughnessy 'Himself,' hovering nearby, interjected, 'I'll vote for her.'

5

Lindsey Chases a Ghost

The hotel lobby rose twenty-four stories into a towering atrium. Wild tales, perhaps apocryphal, were told of clouds forming at its apex, on occasion condensing and raining on startled guests hundreds of feet below.

There was nothing apocryphal about the spectacular view of Monterey Bay as seen from the revolving restaurant and lounge atop the hotel. Tonight a full moon reflected off the black surface of the bay. The lights of Santa Cruz twinkled in the distance.

Hobart Lindsey and Artemis Jansen sat side by side facing a white-jacketed bartender. His steel-gray hair was combed over his ears and curved over his forehead in Beatles-era bangs. He wore dark-rimmed glasses, their arms disappearing behind each ear into a heavy cord. A big Joe

Stalin mustache covered his upper lip. A polished brass rectangle pinned to his jacket read, *Waldemar*.

'Yes, folks, you in town with the conference? What can I get you?'

Artie Jansen pointed to a bottle behind the bartender and said something that sounded like, 'Leapfrog, neat.'

The bartender nodded and smiled. He turned away, brought up the bottle and an empty glass and poured for Artie. 'A pleasure, ma'am. I don't get to pour *Leapfrog* for many customers.' At least, it sounded like *Leapfrog*. Lindsey waited for Waldemar to upright the bottle and read the label.

Laphroiag.

Like a Hebrew restoring the scrolls of the Torah to the Ark, Waldemar placed the bottle of Laphroiag on the mirrored shelf behind him.

Lindsey said, 'What's that, Artemis?'

Artie Jansen lifted her glass and held it beneath her nose. She was tall and big-boned and favored flowing chiffon. Ninety-nine women out of a hundred her size and weight would have looked fat in chiffon. Artie Jansen looked like a Greek statue come to life. 'World's finest scotch.'

Lindsey watched as she dipped the tip of her tongue in the dark brown liquor, then put the glass down with a sigh. 'You're welcome to taste but you may not like it.'

'I'm game.'

'I know you are. That's one of your finer points, Bart.'

He hefted the glass, turned to gaze out over the bay, catching the lights of the seacoast town in the liquor, then took a tentative sip. He put the glass down, grimacing.

'That's what I thought,' Artie grinned. The bartender, watching the exchange, mirrored her expression. The liquor, Lindsey thought, tasted like dark woodsmoke that had been concentrated into a fluid and strained through rich, black peat.

To the bartender Lindsey said, 'I'll have a mineral water, thanks just the same.'

A tall blond man in the uniform of a Confederate officer climbed onto the barstool just beyond Artie. He turned toward Artie and Lindsey and introduced himself. 'John Carter, Captain, Army of the Confederacy. At your service, sir and madame.' When Waldemar had served Lindsey's mineral water Captain Carter signaled and ordered. He turned away to converse with a nearly naked, bright red woman who wore a glittering diadem on her elaborately coifed jet-black hair.

Waldemar returned to Artie Jansen and Lindsey. Leaning close he said, 'They're with the conference, no question there.'

Artie said, 'So are we. Or I am, at least. Bart's just along for the ride. I grew up on Edgar Rice Burroughs. Always wanted to be La, Queen of Opar. That Jane Porter was such a Goody Two-Shoes, I couldn't stand her. Well, what do you expect with a preacher for a pa. But La, now she knew how to live!'

When Waldemar laughed the gray hairs of his mustache fluttered in the breeze. 'Town's full of Tarzans and Janes, John Carters and Dejah Thorises. I even saw a David Innes and a Dian the Beautiful today.'

'You know your Burroughs, then.'

'Read all the books when I was a kid. Doesn't everybody? But some of these people — they think it's gospel truth. Kind of spooky, if you ask me.'

A waitress signaled and Waldemar moved away to fill a drink order.

Artie Jansen swung around on her barstool to get a better view of the bay. Lindsey followed suit. 'You don't find the Burroughs Believers surprising?'

Lindsey laughed. 'I don't think I'd find anything surprising any more. In the business I'm in I've seen people who would kill over an old comic book or a candy dispenser. Why would people astonish me by dressing up in costume and playing games once a year?'

'Right.' Artie downed half her Laphroiag.

'Now that,' Lindsey said, 'I find surprising. How come you like that stuff?'

She shook her head. 'It's an acquired taste. Not like books about the Princess of Mars or the Queen of Opar. I was hooked on those from the start. Even before I could read. We had a set of the old books around the house and I used to stare at those St. John paintings for hours, imagining that I was the beautiful ladies in the pictures. It was really great to be a kid.'

Lindsey said, 'Yes, but we're grown up now, aren't we?'

Artie downed the rest of her drink. 'Maybe.' She paused. 'You want to grab some grub, Bart?'

He nodded. The drink tab was already lying on the polished wood. He dropped a bill on it, including a generous tip in the payment. 'We could eat in the hotel.'

Artie shook her head. 'Let's get out of here. I don't come to a town like Monterey to eat hotel food. Let's sample the local fare.'

Crossing the hotel lobby they passed a snack-and-beverage bar. Weirdly dressed men and women, most of them showing amazing amounts of unnaturally tinted flesh, milled around waving their arms and hollering.

A gaudy banner hung overhead. Gracefully formed if gaudily colored swatches of satin were lovingly stitched to it. Gold, dark green, deep crimson. In large letters

141

they read, BARSOOM BARROOM, and beneath, in smaller script, *Ras Thavas, Prop.*

Outside the hotel, Calle Alvarado was bustling with tourists and conventioneers. You could tell the visitors from the locals. Out of towners, even those from as nearby as San Francisco, had a slightly overdressed look. They might affect tee-shirts and jeans but there was no mistaking them for the local residents with their ever-so-slightly scruffier outfits.

Mostly, Lindsey mused, it was their shoes. The out-of-towners all wore new, clean shoes. They might affect hiking boots or exercise sneakers or brogans or pumps, but they all looked clean and new. Most of the locals looked as if they'd walked all the way from Salinas.

Lindsey and Artie Jansen wound up in an abandoned fire station, now an upscale eatery. The old brick walls had been scrubbed clean and decorated with taste-fully placed prints of flowers and shoots. Artificial clouds hung from the high ceiling. They served double duty as sound baffles and postmodern sculpture.

Over an appetizer of cold asparagus Artie Jansen gave Lindsey an off-center look. 'You're a peculiar one.'

'What?'

'When I invited you down here for the BB's Fest you wanted no part of it. Remember?'

He nodded.

'Not that I didn't try to talk you into it. You just wouldn't leave the Bay Area. You always were the champion stick-in-the-mud in our gang.'

'That isn't fair.' He picked up the wine list and signaled to a waiter. He asked Artie what she'd like and she said a Chardonnay and he ordered a good one. To Artie he said, 'I get around. Hey, I may not be the world traveler you are, but I've worked cases in Chicago and New York, in Louisiana and even in Rome. And I lived in Colorado for a couple of years. I was glad to get home, I won't deny it, but I wouldn't call that being a stick-in-the-mud.'

'Okay, okay,' she grinned. 'What's odd was how all of a sudden you consented to come down here after you said you didn't want to.' She waited for an answer, and when she got none she added, 'I'd almost think you had an ulterior motive.' Another pause, another silence. 'That's it, isn't it? I know you're not just pursuing my delectable charms. You know you could have those back in Oakland or wherever you want them.'

She tilted her head and grinned more widely. 'Bart, you're blushing!'

'All right.' He kept his voice low, glanced at nearby tables. At one a roughneck in cowboy drag and a figure in *faux* gold Samurai armor shared a table with a stunning young woman in perfect 1920's rich girl accoutrement. 'Just a feeling I had.'

The waiter brought their wine and poured a ceremonial dollop for Lindsey. He nodded approval and the waiter filled their glasses. They ordered their dinners. Lindsey had a lamb chop with mint sauce, baby potatoes and spinach. Artie ordered an escarole and arugula salad.

Lindsey raised his eyebrows. 'That's all you're having?'

'Slimming, my dear.' When the waiter

was out of earshot she leaned forward. A tiny diamond in her cleavage caught candlelight and reflected it. 'What about that feeling?'

'You remember that jewel heist down here a couple of years ago?'

'How could I forget it? It's hard to get into those mansions on the Seventeen Mile Drive. Too many millionaires around with their expensive security systems and their private cops.'

'But somebody got into the Eckler house and got away with a major haul. An important diamond ring, a spectacular Burmese ruby necklace, and an exquisite miniature Caravaggio nude that Bill Gates himself tried to buy. Old Eckler just laughed at him.'

'Jewel heist, Bart? Major haul? I love it when you talk crook.' She leaned back and sipped at her Chardonnay. From concealed speakers came the sound of Gonzalo Rubalcava playing Cuban flavored piano. The volume was tastefully low; conversationalists were not forced to raise their voices to be heard.

'I thought they got a picture of the

culprit,' Artie added.

'Right. A good one.' Lindsey laid down his silverware and extracted his International Surety pocket organizer from an inside pocket. He pressed a stud to pop it open. It was a far cry from the scuffed pad and pencil he'd used early in his career. He hit a few keys and handed the organizer to Artie.

'Very impressive.' She looked at an enhanced still lifted from a surveillance tape. It showed a tall Caucasian male with thick dark hair worn Elvis-style. He wore a black tee shirt with a face emblazoned on the chest. The letters of a slogan circled the face. The photo also showed enough of his hands and arms to indicate that he was wearing gloves.

'Can you zoom in on the shirt, Bart?'

He took back the organizer and hit a few more keys.

Artie shook her head at the new version of the picture. ' 'Ross Perot for President. Talk to Me. I'm All Ears.' Very funny.'

'International Surety shelled out plenty of dollars for that one.'

'I'd think it would be easy to find the

thief with that good a photograph.'

'Yes, you would think so, wouldn't you?'

'But they never caught him.'

'Nope.'

She speared a veined red leaf from her plate and studied it. 'Probably a thousand miles away, living it up in Puerto Vallarta or maybe Vancouver.'

'More likely hiding out in Memphis with a gang of Elvis impersonators.' Lindsey bisected a tiny potato, dipped half in mint sauce and chewed it carefully.

'Then why are you in Monterey, Bart?' Artie tilted her head.

Lindsey hesitated. Then he leaned forward. 'I don't really think he's in Memphis. I think he's right here. In this town.'

'That's silly! They'd catch him in a minute.'

'Not if they didn't recognize him.'

'You mean he's going around in a disguise?'

'No. I think he wore a disguise to commit the crime. He must have known that Eckler had a security system. In fact, we're sure he knew, because he did a good job of disabling it. If he hadn't, he'd never have made it out of the mansion with the goods. But he missed one camera. That's how we got the photo and that's how we're going to catch the rascal.'

The piano music ended and the sound of Arturo Sandoval's trumpet filled the interstices of conversation.

Artie pointed to Lindsey's jacket. The pocket organizer was safely stowed. 'He wore a disguise. You mean the pompadour and the sideburns are phony?'

'Maybe. Maybe not.' Lindsey shrugged. 'Probably not, I think.' He lifted his wineglass and looked around the restaurant. It was full now. Most of the tables were occupied by well-dressed couples or groups, but odd-looking celebrants from the Burroughs Fest were scattered here and there.

'What I think,' Lindsey said, 'is that he was a local guy who left town for a couple of years, grew the Elvis hair, came back and did his trick. The local cops knew that if they didn't nab him fast he'd be gone. They tried to catch him leaving town but he never left town. He slipped into a little bolt-hole, shaved off the sideburns, washed the goose-grease out of his pompadour, got rid of his shirt and gloves and turned up again, his old self. If anybody asked, he'd been living in LA or Bakersfield or wherever, and he just got back.'

'And he hasn't turned up in two years? Nor any of the loot? If he didn't get out of the country he must be dead. He's probably at the bottom of a ravine, and the loot with him.'

'Most doubtful. If he's dead, then I'm chasing his ghost. I'm chasing his ghost and I'm going to catch him.'

'Very nice.' Artie locked eyes with Lindsey. 'A very nice theory, I mean. So what if you're right, if he's still alive? We only know what he *doesn't* look like. Is that all you have?'

Lindsey shook his head.

Artie said, 'What's the cat-who-ate-the-canary grin for?'

He brought the organizer back from its home and popped the lid once more. He punched some buttons. 'Take a look at this.'

A different face peered from the organizer screen. Short hair, smooth cheeks, what looked like a chambray work shirt.

'We got the software from a cosmetics outfit. Best thing to hit corporate investigations since DNA testing.'

'You think that's what he looks like now? And he's here in Monterey? Is that why we're here?'

'International Surety paid Mr. Eckler a lot of money for the items he lost. If we could recover the loot he'd be happy to buy it back from us. And he'd have to — under the terms of his policy.'

'What if he's spent the money?'

This time Lindsey laughed out loud. 'Abner Alonzo Eckler? He's richer than Croesus! Don't worry about that, Artie. No. If we could recover those jewels and that painting, even if we had to pay a sizable part of their value for them, we'd come out way ahead once we'd returned them to Eckler and got our settlement back.'

They left the restaurant and strolled along the old streets of California's onetime capital city. An evening mist had moved in from the bay and seabirds called to one another in the moist, cold air. Artie Jansen pulled a heavy shawl around her shoulders and she and Lindsey headed for their hotel.

★　★　★

Artie Jansen rolled over and punched Bart Lindsey in the ribs. 'Hop to, Snakehips! Let's grab a quick shower and get cracking.' She hesitated for a millisecond, then added, 'Unless you'd rather try a little roll in the hay to start the day.'

Lindsey blinked, sat up and yawned. Outside the window the sky was sparkling blue. A few leisurely clouds drifted by. Sea lions were barking in the harbor and the clear air carried the sound across much of the small city.

Lindsey shook his head, as much in astonishment as in drowsiness. He looked at Artie and smiled. She laid her hand on his cheek and smiled back at him. She slid the hand downward playfully but he rotated on his rump and slipped his feet over the edge of the heavy Victorian bed, onto the darkly patterned carpet.

'You're right,' Artie smiled. She inclined her head toward the bedside clock. She reached over and canceled the alarm. 'It would have gone off in another five minutes anyway.' She stood upright. Her thin lime-colored nightgown was transparent against the sunlight streaming through their window.

Lindsey found himself wondering, far from the first time, how he had wound up some hundred-odd miles from home in this beautifully restored Victorian room with Artemis Jansen. The Burroughs Believers Fest had overflowed Monterey's main — and most modern — hotels and they had wound up in this marvelous nineteenth century caravansary. The management even offered a light breakfast — gratis — and milk and cookies at bedtime.

Lindsey and Artie Jansen had been high school classmates more years ago than either cared to remember. Even as a teenager Artie had been an independent spirit and Lindsey had been, he now admitted to himself, a timid soul.

Artie had ventured from suburban Walnut Creek to Berkeley during the Free Speech riots, to San Francisco for the Summer of Love and the psychedelic be-ins of the 1960s, back to Oakland during the Black Panther insurrection.

And Lindsey had gone straight home from school to try and keep his emotionally fragile, widowed mother from going off the rails altogether.

Artie had lived for years in Italy, in Lebanon, and in Singapore, or so she claimed. She'd been married twice, she told Lindsey, or was it three times? And she had a grown-up daughter, Danny, short for Abundanzia, so named, according to Artemis, at the behest of her father, a millionaire Italian count to whom Artie had not then (or ever) been married. Artie had turned up with her daughter in tow at the wedding of Lindsey's mother to Gershon Slonimsky, aka Gordon Sloane, and made herself the center of a storm of energy.

Lindsey had been at the end of a long

involvement with a female homicide detective, the only serious one in his life save for his relationship with his mother, and Artemis Jansen had blasted him out of orbit. He hadn't called Artie in the days following the wedding, as she'd invited him to do, but their paths crossed again, and then again.

A less trusting man than Hobart Lindsey might have suspected that their meetings were not coincidental.

And now they were sharing a room and a bed.

Lindsey dried himself and pulled open the bathroom door. Artie Jansen patted him affectionately and planted a kiss on his freshly shaved cheek as she brushed past him. He caught one more glance of her as she stripped off her nightgown and stepped into the glass-doored shower.

Eric Coffman, Lindsey's lawyer and longtime friend, would have called Artie Jansen *zoftik*. Lindsey preferred *Junoesque*. Whatever the word, Lindsey marveled at the richness of Artie's body and the pleasures she so generously shared with him. He could understand her attracting a series of husbands but he also wondered what had become of them. Artie seemed reluctant to say.

Shortly, over breakfast, they glanced at the day's conference schedule. The Burroughs Believers were an admittedly odd lot. The oddest of them had virtually abandoned their mundane identities and become characters out of Burroughs' various interplanetary yarns or jungle adventures. At the other extreme were academics who regarded Burroughs' works as the epitome of Twentieth Century proletarian literature. They showed up at Believers Fests in their stodgy tweed uniforms and read papers to each other comparing the fauna of Amtor with those of Sasoom or Poloda or Pellucidar, or trying to resolve the infamous Zodanga problem, citing every authority from the scholarly Van Arnam to the words of the Holy Hekkador himself.

Lindsey picked a collectors' panel. His specialty was investigating insurance claims involving collectibles, whether they were garish comic books of the 1940s or classic automobiles of the 1920s or rare, lost motion picture negatives. He slipped into an uncomfortable seat in a converted hotel ballroom. Artie Jansen slid into the chair beside Lindsey's.

Half a dozen Burroughs Believers sat behind a cloth-covered table. Each had a name card in front of him.

The panelists spent half an hour quarreling over the first 1914 McClurg issue of *Tarzan of the Apes*. Did it or did it not have an acorn stamped on the binding cloth? One panelist rose to his feet, lifted a heavy-looking attaché case onto the table, and ostentatiously unlocked its lid. He lifted two plastic-wrapped books from the case and placed them carefully on view. Lindsey squinted. From his seat it appeared that one did have a small acorn on the base of the spine.

'I left the dust jackets at home,' the panelist explained. 'There's no dispute there. Now, as to the question of order of issue . . . '

An hour later the discussion ended except for a few collectors who clustered around the two copies of *Tarzan of the Apes* shouting at each other and waving their fists in the air.

Lindsey and Artie Jansen bought lunch from a falafel vendor in the plaza near the convention center.

The afternoon session was devoted to a slide show and video display of Pathfinder images from Mars. The Believers insisted that the true name of the planet was Barsoom and that its many inhabitants — red, green, white, black, or yellow, four-limbed or six-limbed — had simply laid low to avoid premature discovery. They didn't want to invite a massive invasion from Jasoom — or earth — that they would have had to fight off with their radar-sighted radium rifles and razor-sharp longswords.

Lindsey and Artie Jansen were back at the revolving lounge in time for a snack and libation before the evening's highlight, a costume pageant. They reclaimed their barstools from the previous evening. Waldemar the bartender greeted them with a nod, his steel-gray Joe Stalin mustache looking bushier than ever.

Artie ordered her Laphroiag neat again. Lindsey felt adventurous and chose a local beer. The lounge featured it on tap and Waldemar drew a tall glass for Lindsey before performing his sacred ceremony with Artie's short glass and the dark bottle of Laphroiag. Lindsey had changed to a dark blazer, Oxford-cloth shirt and a maroon knitted tie. Artie favored a revealing teal blouse under a pearl-gray jacket and black trousers.

When the drinks arrived Lindsey reached inside his jacket and extracted his electronic organizer. He set the organizer on the polished wood and punched up a screen that he'd showed Artie the previous evening. Together they studied the image, then looked up at Waldemar.

'Slick gadget you've got there.' Waldemar leaned forward, trying to get a peek at the electronic screen. Lindsey turned the organizer so he could see it.

The bottle slipped from Waldemar's hands and crashed to the floor behind the bar. A rich, earthy-smoky odor arose. Artie Jansen moaned, 'Oh, no!'

Waldemar grabbed Lindsey's organizer and stared at the image. The crash of the bottle had silenced conversation throughout the lounge; now, gradually, the sound of men's and women's voices resumed.

'I suppose this file is just a copy,' Waldemar rasped.

'I'm afraid so.'

Waldemar shook his head. 'Should have known, should have known.'

'Where's the loot?' Lindsey demanded. His voice, normally gentle and unassertive, was suddenly hard. Not loud, just hard.

'Show me tin,' Waldemar hissed.

'I'm no cop.'

'Then who are you?'

Lindsey flashed his International Surety identification.

Waldemar relaxed visibly but at the same time his bushy gray eyebrows drew together in puzzlement. 'What do you want?'

'You still have everything?'

'What do you want?'

'Why are you working at this job?' Lindsey indicated the restaurant with a jerk of his head.

'Why do you think? I have to buy groceries.'

'That's all?'

'That's all.'

'No family?'

'Wife's dead.'

'No one else?'

Waldemar lowered the organizer slowly. He drew a leather wallet from his black bartender's trousers and opened it. He laid it on the bar. Lindsey could feel Artie Jansen at his side as he leaned forward. The girl in the photograph was exquisite.

'How old is she?'

'Fifteen.'

Lindsey exhaled. 'You don't want to go to prison, amigo.'

Waldemar inhaled audibly. He pursed his lips and blew his breath out through his Joe Stalin mustache. 'What do you want?'

'Your girl headed for college?'

'If I could afford to send her. I thought I could swing it before my wife got sick. Thought the insurance would cover that, too. I must have been brain-dead. Damned hospital took every cent we had and then they sent her home to die.' He lifted his dark-framed glasses with both hands and let them fall against his chest. They hung there from their heavy ribbon.

'Sure as hell won't be able to send her to college if I'm in Folsom.'

Lindsey nodded. He turned to Artie Jansen. 'This conversation never happened, understand?'

Artie nodded.

Behind them the restaurant and lounge had cleared out. It was early for the place to be deserted but it was time for the Burroughs Believers' costume gala and those who weren't participating as fantasy characters were eager to get places where they could see those who were.

'You want to stay a free man, Waldemar, and you want to send your girl to college. Abner Alonzo Eckler still wants his trinkets back and my company can recover a lot of money for a modest investment if you'll sell everything back to us.'

'And then you bust me? Not likely.'

'Listen,' Lindsey hissed, 'if I wanted to bust you I'd have a couple of plainclothes cops in this room right now. And I'd have every word you've said on tape. Look.' He leaned back and opened his woolen blazer. The only bulge beneath his shirt

161

was his slightly protruding belly. 'No wire, okay?'

Waldemar said, 'Okay.'

Lindsey pulled a gold International Surety pen from his jacket, wrote a number on a bar napkin and slid it toward Waldemar.

The bartender's eyebrows shot up. 'You'll pay that for the Eckler goods?'

'That's a standard percentage of what we paid Eckler. We get our money back, we come out way ahead. You walk. No questions asked.'

'The diamond and the painting. I couldn't fence them. Everybody said they were great merchandise but they were too hot to handle.'

'What about the ruby?'

'That's gone. Fenced.'

'No it isn't.' Lindsey shook his head.

'It is. I spent the money on medicine for my wife.'

'No, amigo. You still have the ruby. If you'd fenced it, I'd know.'

Waldemar seemed to shrink. 'I can't include it. I can't. You'll see why.'

Lindsey said, 'I don't understand that.'

Waldemar backed away from the bar. He turned toward the kitchen and called, 'Relief.'

In a few minutes a substitute bartender arrived. This one was a hefty middle-aged woman with a twinkle in her eye. 'Good night, Waldy, what happened here? The Laphroiag? That'll come out of your salary, you poor sap!'

'Never mind. I'm gone for the night.' He disappeared from behind the bar.

Artemis Jansen grasped Lindsey's sleeve. 'Where's he going? Hadn't you better call for help?'

'He won't run out. You'll see.'

Waldemar reappeared on the customer side of the mahogany. He'd dispensed with his short bartender's jacket and replaced it with a tweed blazer. 'Let's go downstairs.'

He led them through the hotel's back passages to the ballroom. They emerged in a backstage area and made their way to the wings of the stage. They were in time for the crowning of the Jeddak and Jeddara of the Burroughs Believers.

The Jeddak was a massive man with

convincing green skin, foot-long tusks and an extra pair of limbs. He was introduced as Tardos Mors, Jeddak of Greater Helium, to a loud round of applause.

The Jeddara was introduced as Tara of Helium, daughter of John Carter and Dejah Thoris, but Lindsey recognized her instantly as the young woman whose picture Waldemar carried in his wallet. She wore a minimal costume. Her skin was a deep red, the result of skillfully applied body makeup. Her figure was slim, no more developed than the average fifteen-year-old's, but there was a symmetry in her face and a grace in her carriage that drew every eye to her.

A slim gold chain circled her neck, and on her youthful bosom a fabulous, dark red ruby gleamed in the light of a single baby spot.

Lindsey heard Waldemar's voice in his ear. 'Her mother looked like that.'

Artie Jansen shook her head. 'Pardon me for butting in, but I couldn't help overhearing. Are we talking about a child bride? If your wife looked like that, Waldemar . . . '

164

The bartender, now in civilian garb, looked annoyed. 'Our parents were neighbors and best friends. We grew up together. They gave us baths together when we were toddlers. We started school together. We knew we'd be married some day. And, yes, her mother looked like that when we were in middle school. I look at her sometimes and I still cry.'

Lindsey said, 'The diamond and the Caravaggio. Abner Eckler will settle. Too bad you fenced the ruby, but Abner will settle for the diamond and the Caravaggio.'

★   ★   ★

'I'll say this for expense accounts, Bart, they certainly let you eat in interesting establishments.'

'Not a great salary, but the perks are nice,' Lindsey conceded.

They'd shared a cocktail, then begun their meal with cured salmon hors d'oeuvres and onion soup. A basket of warm rolls adorned their table, beside a candle in a silver holder.

For entrées Artie Jansen permitted herself a petit filet mignon and scampi combination. Lindsey chose the house paella. A combination of saffron rice, Monterey Bay seafood, spicy sausage, peas, green onions, red and green bell peppers.

As their waiter poured their wine, a South African Dornier Stellenbosch, Artie put her hand on Lindsey's wrist. 'I hope I wasn't out of line, Bart.'

He raised an eyebrow. In the flickering candlelight it gave him a satanic look. He waited for her to elaborate.

'I mean — about that child bride business.'

'No, it was a sensible question.'

'I mean, when a girl goes from a skinny stick to a mature woman in a few years, it's a big experience.'

'I can imagine.'

'I doubt it. I know boys change, too, but it isn't the same. I had brothers, I know what they went through. It was nothing compared to being a girl.'

Lindsey speared a baked clam from his paella, sliced it in half and downed it with

166

a sip of Dornier. 'I remember watching the girls in school.' He smiled wistfully.

'But — I'm afraid I upset Waldemar.'

'He took it in stride. After all, he's a bartender. They have to deal with all types.'

'But, Bart — ' she sliced a corner of filet, dipped it in rich sauce, chewed meditatively.

Lindsey waited.

'I don't understand why you let him get away with that ruby. It must be worth a fortune. And it makes you an accessory, doesn't it? Couldn't you wind up doing time?'

'I suppose so.' He didn't seem worried.

'Well, I certainly won't blow the whistle on you.'

'I never thought you would.' He let his glance drift around the interior of the restaurant. It was fashioned like a Belgian country inn, with dark, heavy timbers, stucco walls, a huge brick fireplace warming the room against the chilly northern California night.

'You don't have to explain yourself.'

'No, I don't.'

'But if you wouldn't mind . . . ' She lifted her glass again. Dancing firelight reflected from her eyes and from her wine.

Lindsey reached for a roll, broke off a chunk and dabbed it with butter. The crust was crisp; the interior of the roll gave off steam. He took a while to gather his thoughts, then breathed a sigh.

'I've always played by the book, Artie. In my business there are a lot of temptations. I won't deny that I've thought about cutting corners a few times. There are plenty of insurance rackets.'

'I've heard.'

'But this one — maybe this is going to be my last hurrah, I don't know. How long do we carry around our dirty baggage? There are statutes of limitations in the law, you know. A man or a woman goes bad, screws up, learns a lesson, straightens himself out. You live a decent life for decades, and then some beast rises out of his past and bites you. Is that right? Maybe it is, maybe we still need to pay for our mistakes. But then we talk about redemption, and — '

He stopped and shook his head. 'Who the hell am I to babble about this? Look — '

Artemis Jansen waited, her expression expectant.

Lindsey said, 'Couldn't you see how much that poor man loved his wife? Couldn't you see the grief? His daughter is everything to him. We'll get back the painting and the diamond. Abner Eckler will be happy. International Surety will cut its loss, they'll be happy. That girl will have the gem, and someday, who knows, it will pay for her college education.'

'So you think you're doing the right thing, Bart?'

'Artie, I'm trying. That's all I can do. That's all I can think of to do. I'm trying.'

6

News From New Providence

His royal robes were heavy, heavy. And so
hot! Why was it so hot in the Cathedral?
It was only June. Why could the
Archbishop not complete the crowning
and the anointing, the blessing of the
monarch, the placement of scepter and
orb? Then he would present his Queen
Consort to the nation and the empire and
be damned to the PM and the rotten
dog-collared clergy, that bloodless super-
annuated fool Cosmo Lang, and —

— and suddenly he was looking up at
the high ceiling above his bed, where the
broad blades of a slowly-turning fan
could do little more than stir the hot,
moist air of this damned backwater
island. The dream was gone, the dream
that had come and gone so many times,
and he was King no longer. He was
Governor-General of a string of rocky

protuberances that poked out of this Caribbean backwater and gave home to a couple of thousand colonial expatriates, white chicken farmers and black fisherman.

And his aide was standing just inside the doorway of the bedroom fidgeting like a schoolboy and clearing his throat desperately to get the Duke's attention.

He pushed himself upright in bed. His silk pyjamas, the lightest pair he owned, were stained with perspiration. The tropical sun beat through window curtains and turned the room into a blaze of daylight.

The Duke reached for a cigarette, struck flame from a lighter embossed with his coat of arms, and drew in a deep draught of smoke. 'Yes, Deering?'

'Something terrible, sir.' Deering shifted his weight from foot to foot. He still carried the rank of colonel in the guards but he maintained a wardrobe of mufti at the Duke's suggestion. 'Something terrible has happened.'

'Well?'

'It's Sir Walter, sir. Sir Walter Maples. At The Tradewinds, sir.'

'Thank you, Deering, I know quite well the name of Sir Walter's home. The Duchess and I stayed there at one time, you will remember.'

'Yes, sir.'

The Duke drew on his cigarette, waiting for Deering to go on. The dream came every night now, or so it seemed. It left him high-strung and unrested each morning and a cigarette helped to calm his nerves.

'Sir Walter, sir — '

'Spit it out, Deering.'

'He's dead, sir.'

The Duke hesitated for a split second. Then, 'Who knows?'

'His houseman found him, sir.'

'Oh, that fellow, yes. What's his name?'

'Plum, sir. Stolid black chap. Not too bright an individual. Skin the color of his name. Marcus Plum, I believe it is.'

'Who else?'

'Sir Walter was alone, sir. Lady Margarethe is off the island. In Canada with her daughter. The only other white man in the house was Mr. Harrel. Plum fetched him and — '

'Her Royal Highness has not been disturbed, I hope.'

'No, sir. As soon as Mr. Easton — '

'You didn't tell me that Easton knew.'

'Beg pardon, sir. It seems that Mr. Harrel telephoned the commissioner as soon as Plum sounded the alarm. Mr. Easton felt that the Governor-General should be informed at once.'

'Well, very rightly so, Deering, very rightly so.'

'Yes, sir.'

The Duke climbed out of bed. He drew one final puff on his cigarette and crushed out the butt in a massive cut-glass ashtray. He smoothed his rumpled pyjamas, running his hands down the silken legs.

'Close the door, will you, Deering? No need to waken the household.'

'Yes, sir.' Deering complied.

The Duke stepped into his lavatory and doffed his pyjama shirt. 'All right, Deering, I can hear you from in here. You were saying — ?'

While his aide spoke, the Duke filled a glass with fresh tap water, wetted his toothbrush and sprinkled tooth-cleansing powder on its bristles. He gave his teeth a thorough brushing. Having rinsed his mouth, he instructed Deering to provide a step-by-step review of the sad events at The Tradewinds.

'It's unfortunate that we have to rely on the Negro's version, sir.'

'Nevertheless, Deering, nevertheless.'

'Yes, sir. Yes. Well, apparently Sir Walter indicated that he wanted to spend the day fishing.'

The Duke shook his head. 'Indicated how, Deering? To whom? You must be specific.'

'I apologize, sir. I assume that Sir Walter would have spoken with Plum the pervious evening. Last evening, sir.'

'Are you unaware, Deering, that Sir Walter hosted a small dinner last night in honor of Her Highness and myself, at The Tradewinds?'

'No, sir.'

'No?' The Duke raised an eyebrow. 'No, you were unaware? Or no, you were not unaware?'

'Sorry, sir. I meant to say that, no, sir, I

am not unaware of that fact. That is, I am quite aware that the Governor and Her Royal Highness dined at The Tradewinds. As I recall, sir, the guest list was quite small, just Sir Walter Maples, Mr. Harrel, Count Grenner, and Sir Walter's son-in-law, M. Delacroix. Her Royal Highness was the only lady present.'

Of course. The Duchess was at her best surrounded by male admirers who sought her favor and attention. She did not care for female companionship; it smacked inevitably of competition.

'Yes, M. Delacroix,' the Duke said. 'Why the Vichy authorities didn't slap him in irons, I shall never understand. Or turn him over to the Germans. The Gestapo would know how to deal with M. Antoine Delacroix, you can rest assured of that, Deering.'

Deering ran his finger around his collar uncomfortably. He wished he could switch to clothing more suited to the climate of these islands, but the Duke was adamantly opposed to the relaxation of Britannic propriety. More likely, Deering thought, it was the Duchess' iron will rather than the Duke's adherence to tradition that was at play.

He suppressed a sigh.

The Duke asked, 'Who else, Deering? You said that Commissioner Easton, Harrel and this Negro, Plum, know about Maples. Who else?'

'That's all, sir.'

'Well, why the devil didn't Easton telephone me? Why didn't he come straight to Government House and inform me? Who does he think he is, some ha'penny gumshoe? Who does he think I am?'

Deering bit back an impulse to answer the question and instead waited for the Duke to continue. But the Duke emerged from the lavatory wrapped in a heavy chenille robe.

'Damned place, damned job, can't even get a reliable dresser to tend to my needs. Deering, fetch me an outfit from the wardrobe and be quick.' The Duke gestured, then waited for Deering to select a medium tan silken shirt, regimental tie, pleated trousers and light linen jacket. He dressed carefully but swiftly, knotting the tie in the pattern he had

176

himself invented and that bore his name worldwide — his personal contribution to sartorial posterity.

'One thought that His Royal Highness might see fit to take a personal hand in the case,' Deering ventured.

'Yes, certainly, capital idea. I shall want to speak with Commissioner Easton first.'

'Yes, sir. And I thought His Highness might wish to question Mr. Harrel and the houseman, Plum, as well.'

'Why in the world would I want to — oh, you did say that he found Sir Walter's, ah, remains, did you not? Well, I suppose it might be a good idea. Deering, you'll have to learn to order your thoughts, don't you know? You're much too confused to deal with a crisis such as this. Well, get Easton on the telephone. Have him come here at once. Bring Harrel, of course, and that black fellow. Where is he? Where is Easton? I suppose I must break the news to the Duchess. I don't know how she's going to take this.'

Deering stepped out of the Duke's path, bowing slightly as the Duke brushed past him.

The Duke tapped gently on the door to the Duchess's boudoir. He pressed his ear to the tropical wood. Was that a slight stirring? He tapped again. 'Are you awake, my darling? May I enter?'

After a lengthy silence he heard her muttering. He scampered back to his own quarters. Deering was using the telephone. The Duke signaled to his aide. Deering uttered a few more syllables and lowered the instrument. 'Yes, sir.'

'See to it that the Duchess has her tea and toast. I don't understand this household, can't keep up the most elementary level of service.'

Deering flushed. 'At once, sir.'

The Duke waited outside the Duchess's chambers until a servant approached bearing Her Highness's breakfast tray. 'I'll take that.' The Duke carried the tray into the boudoir and placed it carefully on the bed, its folding legs holding it at a level comfortable for Her Highness.

She sipped at the tea, swallowed and lowered the cup. The china was of course imported from England and bore the Ducal crest. 'Now, David, what is the fuss?'

He looked around for a chair, asked permission to be seated, drew it close to her bedside. 'I have dreadful news, my dear. Sir Walter Maples is dead.'

The Duchess raised her chin. 'Walter? What happened?'

'His houseman found him in his room this morning. Called Chris Harrel, he was staying over at The Tradewinds. Harrel phoned Ray Easton, then phoned here. Deering gave me the news. I hope you won't be too upset, my darling. If there were a way to spare you this I should have done so.'

'But that's terrible, David.' The Duchess nibbled a corner of her toast. 'Absolutely terrible.' She washed the toast down with another sip of tea. 'You've got to tell me everything.'

Before the Duke could answer, Deering rapped his knuckles on the Duchess's door. 'Beg pardon, sir. Madame. Commissioner Easton is here, sir. And Plum.'

'Have them wait in my office downstairs. I shall be there as soon as possible.' He turned back toward the Duchess.

'Has anyone told Margarethe yet?' the

Duchess asked. 'She has to know. Poor thing. All their years together. And she put up with so much from him. You know, David, he was not an easy man. Not easy at all.'

The Duke looked away. 'I shall send your maid up to dress you, my dear.'

'Yes, please.'

As he descended the broad flight of stairs he wondered what his brother was doing at this moment. Adjusting for the difference in time, it would be late in the day in England. The Nazis had refrained from bombing Buckingham Palace for more than a year after the commencement of hostilities, and they might never have attacked, might never have needed to attack, had the Duke remained upon the throne. Had he not allowed himself to be shipped off to this lonely exile. New Providence, Grand Bahama, the rest of the islands of his Lilliputian realm — they might as well be Elba and St. Helena.

Ribbentrop had been quite reasonable, after all. And his boss, Herr Hitler — well, a decidedly peculiar chap. Not a pleasant person, very poor manners. But then what could one expect of an individual with his lowly origins? But their ideas had not been so far apart after all. They recognized the twin perils to Mankind, Bolshevism and Jewry. Why should the great Nordic peoples, the Anglo-Saxons and the Germans, be at each other's throats while the lesser races stood by waiting to pick at their carcasses?

It didn't make sense, and he'd tried to make the politicians see that it didn't make sense, but Baldwin and Chamberlain and Churchill were all such a gang of stiff-necked fools, they either could not or would not recognize the reality that confronted them — and England.

Deering held the door for him as he entered his study. Ray Easton, Christopher Harrel, and the Negro, Plum, had preceded him, per his instructions. When the Duke entered the room Easton sprang to his feet; Harrel rose lazily to his. Plum was already standing. Easton was a big-boned man. He affected a tropical linen suit and plain black tie. Harrel was attired in a colorful shirt, rough trousers and sandals. Hardly proper attire. The Negro wore not a houseman's outfit of black trousers and white jacket but a fisherman's faded trousers and open-necked shirt. He held a battered fisherman's cap in one hand.

The Duke shook his head in despair.

He circled the others and seated himself behind his desk. He waved to Deering and the latter closed the office door, remaining inside.

'Now, what is this about Sir Walter Maples, Commissioner?'

'If I may, sir — '

The Duke gestured Easton to a seat, Harrel to another.

'Plum here found him,' Harrel volunteered. 'Soon as he fetched me I could see poor Walt was as dead as a doornail. Look on his face as if he'd seen a ghost. More like he is one, now, eh? Blood spattered all over the walls, coverlet soaked, what a mess, what a mess.'

'Thank you, Harrel,' the Duke nodded. He kept to himself his opinion of the man, that Harrel was an unspeakable wretch, little better than cockney trash.

But he was one of the colony's wealthiest and most influential citizens, a force in the legislative council. One put up with what one must.

The Duke asked the houseman, 'What have you to say for yourself, Plum?'

The Negro closed his eyes as if gathering his thoughts. He held his fisherman's cap in both hands. He shifted his weight from foot to foot. How like Deering, the Duke thought.

'Well?'

'Sah, Sah Walter ask me last night. Your Highness and Her Highness takes your partings and leaves Tradewinds for Government House and he ask me, can I take him out this morning. Early, fo' sunrise.'

'Yes. And did he say what the destination was to be?'

'Chub Cay, sah.'

'Chub Cay?' The Duke appeared startled.

'Yes, sah. I reckon, we could pick up a nice easterly this time of year, make it to Chub by midmorning, easy.'

The Duke lifted a briar pipe from the

rack on his desk. He held it in one hand and tapped its bowl in the palm of the other. 'Did Sir Walter say what he wanted to do at Chub?'

Plum shook his head from side to side. 'No, sah, he did not. He is my employer, sah, and he is entitled. He was my employer, I should say.'

'Quite. Well, go on, Plum.'

'I woke up and went to Sir Walter's room. I knocked on his do' — '

'What time was this?'

'I don' know the hour, sah. I just know, when I went to bed, I tol' my mind to wake me up good an' early cos' Sir Walter want to get an early start. But he didn't answer my knock, so I went in, Sir Walter's door wasn't locked, and that was when I found him. Sah.'

The Duke returned the pipe to its place in the rack. He slipped a cigarette case from an inside pocket of his jacket, extracted a cigarette and lit it from a heavy lighter before Deering could spring across the room and hold a flame for him.

He blew a plume of smoke into the air. 'Mr. Harrel, what can you add to this?'

'Not much, Your Highness. I was sleepin' like a log.'

'Where is the room in which you were staying?'

'Cross the hall. Down the way from poor old Walt's.'

'Do you stay often at The Tradewinds?'

'After last night I didn't want to drive home. Hard to get petrol these days, eh?'

'Indeed. Well, continue.'

'So Walt, he said he was a bit low on petrol himself so he couldn't drive me home, eh, so put me up in his guest room.'

'This was solely for the purpose of saving petrol?'

'Well, I'll level with you, Governor.'

'Please.'

'I was kind of, well, two or three sheets to the wind. Had a couple of drinks before the meal and a few glasses of wine and a snifter afterwards, Your Highness. So I thought it wasn't such a grand idea to drive, you see.'

'I do indeed. Commendable of you not to risk it. Commendable of Sir Walter to put you up. Were you part of this plan to visit Chub Cay?'

'Not as I can remember.'

'Did you and Sir Walter stay up talking last night?'

'Not as I can remember.'

The Duke turned sharply toward Plum once again. 'You're sure that Sir Walter made no mention of his purpose in visiting Chub Cay? Think hard, Plum.'

The Negro scratched his head. 'I think he might o' said something, sah.'

'Well, and what was that something?' The Duke made an effort to contain his impatience.

'Something about countin' on it, sah.'

'Counting on it?'

'Somethin' like that, sah.'

'It couldn't have been something about the Count, could it? Count Grenner?'

Plum looked as if he was going to explode from the strain of concentrating. He held his breath until his eyes bulged, then exhaled explosively. 'Sir Walter, he might could have said, 'Count When.' I thought he said, 'Count When.' Like when you pourin' a drink fo' yo' frien' and you say, 'Say when,' he might could have said, 'Count When.''

'Thank you, Plum.' The Duke closed his eyes and pondered. He realized now that it might have been better had he questioned Plum in private. Count Max Grenner was to be his partner and front man in the development of Chub Cay. The Duke, Walter Maples, and Count Grenner.

It all had to do with the economy of the colony. The Bahamas had been a sleepy backwater for many years, until the Americans had put in their law prohibiting the manufacture and sale of alcoholic beverages. Then, ah, then the Bahamas had boomed! Whiskey was imported from Britain, schnapps from Germany, wine from Italy. Freighters docked in the Bahamas, their cargo off-loaded onto small, fast craft and smuggled into the States via Florida.

It was saddening to realize that a single slip of the tongue, an exercise of candor when discretion should have dictated a wiser course, could bring one down. There was that American who had parlayed capital raised running rum into a fortune in film production and risen to the Ambassadorship at the Court of St. James, only to be laid low by a single foolish remark regarding the inefficacy of democracy.

The fact that he was right did nothing to alter the circumstances.

The Duke addressed the houseman once more. 'I want you to take me where you were to take Sir Walter.'

Plum said, 'You want to go to Chub Cay, sah?'

'That is correct.'

Plum tilted his head, obviously deep in thought. 'I s'pose I c'd take you, sah. My boat, she's all outfitted. I was plannin' to take Sir Walter this mo'nin', I c'n take you instead, sah.'

'Very well, then.' The Duke stood up. Commissioner Easton leaped to emulate him, Christopher Harrel lazily following suit. 'Easton, Harrel, you will hold yourselves in readiness should I need to question you further. Deering, you may return to your duties. Plum, you shall await me on the verandah of Government House.'

'Yes, sah!'

The others stood, heads slightly inclined,

188

as the Duke strode from the room.

He climbed the broad staircase leading to the family quarters and tapped once more on the Duchess's door. Her familiar voice called out, 'Come!'

He found her within, reclining on a *chaise longue*, garbed in a Mainbocher dressing gown of pale blue silken faille. She wore matching blue mules, each topped by a fluffy cotton pouf. A star sapphire pendant rested against her throat and a cuff of matching stones circled one wrist.

'My darling,' he said.

'Yes, David, what is it?' He observed that her breakfast tray had been removed and the bed straightened.

'I don't suppose, my dear, that you would care for a brief sail today?'

'A sail? You just told me that Walter Maples was dead. And you're going sailing?'

'I am investigating his death, my dear. It appears that he came to a dreadful, bloody end, but he had planned an expedition this morning to Chub Cay and I thought to follow his planned route, don't you see.'

'I see plenty, David. I see you trying to

play Sherlock Holmes. Don't we have our own little Inspector Lestrade on this dreadful island? Can't you leave the investigation to the official police?'

The Duke frowned. 'You forget, my darling, that as Governor-General I am the colony's chief law-enforcement officer.'

'Yes, and you're the commander of its military force, but I don't see you drilling recruits on the parade ground.'

The Duke blinked. Her Royal Highness was in one of her moods. Well, who could blame her? Being awakened to the news of the murder of one's closest friend — well, one of one's closest friends, anyway — would surely put any sensitive person into a state. He drew a breath, waited until he was certain that she was not going to speak further, and resumed.

'Walter was my friend as well as yours, my dear. Not to mention a prospective business associate. This war is not going to last forever, you know. We have to think of the future.'

'You know what our future should have been,' she grumbled bitterly. 'We should be at Belvedere if not Buckingham this very moment instead of that stammering weakling and his simpering little wifey. If you weren't such a fool — '

'Stop it!' He felt the pressure within his head and knew that his face had turned a bright red. Rarely did he stand up to the Duchess, but there was a single topic on which he would not brook her criticism. 'He is my dear brother!'

'And see how he treated you once you had made him Caesar,' came the hissed reply.

'My family is sacred. That is the end of it.'

He spun on his heel and left the room.

He found Plum awaiting him downstairs, standing respectfully near the tall cut-glass doors. The Duchess of course was right. It was such a tragically far cry from Buckingham and Belvedere and the life of pomp and privilege they had known before the abdication, to this hot and isolated post. If only he could go back and change things — but he could not.

'Pardon, Governor sah, but yo' shoes — '

The Duke managed a rueful grin, the

first of the day. Of course. This would be no Mediterranean cruise such as he and the Duchess had shared on the palatial *Nahlin*, nor a Caribbean jaunt like those hosted by Max Grenner aboard *Stella Australis*. What could poor Plum own but a little sailing dinghy?

'Have you suitable footwear for sailing, Plum?'

'Sah, I sails barefoot.'

'Then I shall do the same,' the Duke rejoined, grinning broadly.

They strode side-by-side between the white pillars of Government House, past the Duchess's precious Buick sedan and down sleepy Blue Hill Road toward Prince George's Wharf.

Plum's craft was as the Duke had expected. The Duke removed his shoes, socks and garters and left them on the quay. He waited while Plum climbed into the dinghy. Plum helped him into the boat, cast off the painter, then used a pair of heavy oars to propel the dinghy away from the quay.

Plum raised a much-patched sail, swung the dinghy to port, caught a late-morning breeze and guided the craft through the narrow channel separating Nassau from Hog Island.

A few scrawny goats wandered the hilly island, cropping sparse vegetation. As the dinghy rounded Hog Island and swung to the north, toward Chub Cay, the Duke permitted himself a fantasy. A U-boat would rise from the sparkling turquoise sea. Its captain would emerge from the conning tower, take the Duke onboard and return with him to a subdued Britain where he would resume his temporarily abandoned throne.

He would offer his brother and his consort better treatment than the stammerer had offered him and his wife. That much generosity he could afford. Wrongs would be righted, mistakes would be corrected, injustices would be undone. The rightful king would reign once again!

'They be Chub!'

The Duke abandoned his reverie with reluctance, but there indeed was the Cay where he and his partners had planned to build their resort once the war had ended. When the Americans repealed their prohibition of alcohol they had crushed the booming economy of the Bahamas, but there was another prohibition in the United States, against gambling. It was carried on legally in one of the arid western states, he recalled, and was winked at in the city of Miami.

But a full-scale luxurious casino in the style of Monte Carlo, located in the salubrious surroundings of the Bahamas, would be his bonanza. His and the Duchess's, of course, assuming that she did not abandon him for a fresher and more energetic companion, as she had previously abandoned one husband for a second and that husband for himself. She'd already picked out her fourth mate, the Duke suspected, but that liaison had been scotched, there was no longer any danger from those quarters!

'This where Sah Walter was wantin' to go this mo'nin', sah.' Plum was standing at the tiller, a line in one hand running to the little dinghy's boom. 'You want me to put in, sah?'

The Duke shook his head. 'No, Plum, there will be no need for that. Could you circle the Cay, I'd like to survey it today, then return to port?'

As the man moved to obey, the Duke questioned him. 'You say Sir Walter had bled copiously when you found him, Plum.'

'Sah?'

The Duke blinked. 'You say there was blood spattered all over the room.'

'Yes, sah.'

'I didn't think a bullet to the brain would cause such bleeding.'

'Bullet, sah?'

'Yes. Was Sir Walter not killed by a gunshot?'

The black man shrugged. 'That man's throat be slashed and his belly sliced open. Whoevah done in Sir Walter was one mean person. I didn't see no bullet hole, sah.'

After a moment the Duke asked, 'Do you sleep at The Tradewinds, Plum?'

'No, sah.' Plum shook his head. 'I go home every night to sleep, I come back to The Tradewinds every mo'nin'.'

'So you would not have heard a gunshot. And Chris Harrel was drunk.'

Beating back through Nassau Harbor, the Duke half expected to see Max Grenner's *Stella Australis* moving majestically toward the open sea, but she was nowhere to be seen, nor was she tied up at Grenner's usual dockage. Come to think of it, the grand yacht had not been at her place when the Duke left Prince George's Wharf hours earlier with the Negro Plum.

Once again shod, the Duke returned to Government House and telephoned the Harbor Master. He learned that *Stella Australis* had sailed at daybreak. Only the Count and Countess Grenner were on board, aside from the crew, of course. No, sir, the Harbor Master did not know their destination, although he thought it might be either the Count's villa at Tampico or his mansion at Veracruz.

The Duke slammed the telephone down. Damn Grenner! He and Maples had been the main financiers of the planned casino at Chub Cay. The Duke's allowance from the Crown was a precarious pittance, hardly enough to cover the Duchess's clothing budget. And his brother, he knew, was plagued with constant health problems. Should he die the scepter would pass to his elder daughter, and who knew how she would treat himself and the Duchess? They had been close when he was Prince of Wales but cracks had appeared in the family structure during his brief reign and since the abdication he had not seen either of his nieces, nor received as much as a greeting card from them on his birthday.

He had to make a go of the casino! Now that Maples was dead, Max Grenner's role was more important than ever. It was vital.

The dead Walter Maples had come from humble enough roots: a rough diamond prospector he had found a mother lode in South Africa and made his fortune. That would pass now to the detestable Lady Margarethe, maybe even fall into the hands of the son-in-law, the vile Delacroix. There was no counting on that money any longer.

Grenner's fortune was even more unsavory. He maintained his residency in neutral Sweden, built guns and sold munitions to both sides, cash and carry, no questions asked. The Crown was after him, the PM had personally sought his extradition, but the Duke exercised his official prerogatives and gave Grenner free run of the Bahamas.

But what if Grenner had heard of Maples' death early this morning? What if word had spread even before notification reached Government House? Grenner held the exchequer for the planned casino, including the portion put up by the Duke. The amount was modest enough by the standards of the likes of Walter Maples or Max Grenner. The Duke's chief contribution to the scheme was the prestige of his name, the glamour that he and the Duchess would provide to the eventual establishment, that would draw wealthy gamblers from the entire Western Hemisphere if not from Europe. But he had insisted on putting up a share of the capital that represented a huge investment by his standards. Had Grenner decamped for Mexico with all the money?

The Duke raced up the broad staircase

to his wife's boudoir. She was not there.

He found her shortly in the garden, sunning with her terriers. She had changed her costume to a day-frock of cornflower blue linen. A broad-brimmed hat protected her delicate skin from the rays of the sun, and she wore a pair of oversized spectacles of smoked-glass in harlequin frames of jewel-decorated tortoise shell. She was seated beneath an oversized parasol, a cold glass beaded with condensation at her elbow, a novel opened in her lap. She looked up as the Duke literally ran to her.

'What is it, David? You're as pale as a ghost!'

'Where were you last night?' the Duke demanded.

Behind her dark glasses, did he detect a blink? In her always-confident voice, did he hear a hesitation? 'Why, I was with you at dinner, of course. Colonel Deering drove us there in the Buick.'

'Afterwards, afterwards.'

'Why, we returned here, David. What's the matter with you?'

'You did not go out again? You did not

return to The Tradewinds and — and see Walter Maples?'

'David, don't make an ass of yourself. What are you implying?'

'I am implying that you took the Buick. Late at night. Quite late at night. You took a knife from the pantry here at Government House and drove yourself back to The Tradewinds and entered the house. Only Chris Harrel was present, other than Walter Maples, and Harrel was immobilized with liquor. You made your way to the master bedroom. You found Maples dead to the world and with the knife you slashed his throat and belly.'

'David,' the Duchess laughed nervously, 'why would I do such a horrible thing?'

'Because Maples was your lover and he was losing interest in you. You follow the same pattern, my dear, but this time you couldn't simply divorce me and move on. You couldn't continue to satisfy Maples. I know you, I know you now, at last. Perhaps you hoped for a reconciliation but when you couldn't even waken him you flew into a rage and used your knife on him.'

She removed her sunglasses, folded them and placed them in the gutter of the open book in her lap. She glared at him coldly. 'He would not even stir,' she said.

'That was because there was a bullet in his brain already.' The Duke started to walk away, then halted and turned back to face his wife. He stood beside her, aware that to her eyes he was a menacing black silhouette against the blazing Caribbean sun.

'You must have been enraged. You pummeled him and spattered his uncongealed blood around the room. Did you manage to keep it off your gown, or will I find that in your hamper?

'Max Grenner and the Countess are gone. Sailed away with Walter's money,' he paused dramatically, 'and ours.'

She gasped and started to rise.

He placed his hand on her shoulder, pressing her back into her seat. 'It seems that we are fated to remain together for the rest of our lives, my dear. We deserve each other.'

7

Golden Glory

'Chicago again?'

Richelieu nodded.

'We have plenty of good people there,' Lindsey said. 'Why should I fly out there to tackle a case that somebody onsite can take care of?'

Richelieu removed his gold-framed spectacles and turned them in front of his elegant tie. The bright sunlight of a Colorado morning glinted from polished lenses and danced across his immaculate desktop.

'You're thinking of Gina Rossellini?'

'Indeed.'

Richelieu leaned back in his brass-studded leather chair. 'Maybe she could. But this one seems right down your alley. I thought you'd jump at it.'

Lindsey pursed his lips. 'I haven't even seen the case folder, Mr. Richelieu. You're hardly being fair.'

'Of course not. Never have been, have I? Don't intend to start now.' Richelieu grinned.

Lindsey tried to fathom his boss's statement. On the face of it, it was true. Desmond Richelieu had a chew-'em-up-and-spit-'em-out reputation throughout International Surety. But if that was Richelieu's attitude, would he tip his hand so blatantly? Hardly. Unless he was using his mock-duplicity to mask real duplicity. Another of Richelieu's famous infinite recursions.

'Let me study the case and I'll get right back to you.' Lindsey was Richelieu's subordinate, his deputy, and as such he found himself saddled with more and more administrative work and ever fewer opportunities to get into the field and settle cases.

It was frustrating.

Richelieu lifted his telephone from a drawer and purred into it. Before he had put the phone down Mrs. Blomquist arrived with a bright red file folder. Lindsey knew what that color meant.

Richelieu tipped an almost imperceptible gesture and Mrs. Blomquist placed the folder in front of Lindsey, corner perfectly squared to the corner of Richelieu's desk.

'You'll take it,' Richelieu said.

Lindsey carried the folder to his own office. Hours later he strode across the lobby of Denver's bizarre circus tent of an air terminal. He phoned SPUDS-Chicago from the jet. When a voice answered, 'International Surety, Special Projects Unit,' Lindsey asked for Ms. Rossellini.

When Lindsey left the jetway at Midway she was waiting for him. At least he hadn't had to deal with O'Hare.

'So what brings you back to our splendid city in the middle of this lovely heat wave?'

'Mary Joseph.'

Gina Rossellini barked her laughter. 'I had a feeling that one would bring you out.'

'I'm surprised you didn't handle it yourself,' Lindsey replied.

'Never had a chance. The claim went in through the regular I.S. office. I only spotted it on the traffic to Denver. You going solo on this one, or you want some company?'

Lindsey considered briefly. By this time they were in Rossellini's glittering Dodge Viper, immersed in the city's nighttime flow. The sky was black but a nearly full moon seemed to blaze as hot as a minor sun.

'Do you know the case?'

'As well as you do, probably.'

'Better, I'd think. You know Chicago and I'm just a visitor here.'

Gina Rossellini floored the gas pedal and the Viper's big engine roared as she swerved around a monstrous SUV, its pilot more interested in a cell-phone conversation than in maneuvering through the heavy traffic. Gina snorted. 'Yes, I'd like to get into this one.'

'We need to talk it over, then.'

'Over what? Over a cool beverage or over a good meal?'

'I didn't touch the airplane food,' Lindsey smiled. 'Do you have a special joint in mind?'

'My Uncle Aldo's. Best Italian food in Cicero. If you don't mind a little detour.

And we'll get a head start on this case while we're in the neighborhood.'

'Let's do it.'

Shortly Gina pulled the Viper to the curb of Cermak Road in Cicero. The neon sign on the restaurant read, *Aldo's Amber Lantern*. It had the look of an old-style family place. Gina told Lindsey that it had been in this spot since Al Capone's day, and some of the clientele were old enough to have broken bread with Capone.

A white-jacketed valet opened the driver's side door before Gina could turn off the engine. When Lindsey asked if the car would be safe in this neighborhood, Gina said, 'Everybody around here knows my car. And they know Uncle Aldo. Believe me, it's safe.'

The last customers were leaving the Amber Lantern as Lindsey and Rossellini arrived, but the tuxedo-clad *maitre d'* made a half-bow. 'Miss Rossellini.' He nodded to Lindsey. 'Sir.' And back to Gina, 'Your usual table,' and led the way.

A few minutes later they sipped dark Valpolicella and nibbled at antipasto.

Lindsey studied the dark-red flocked wallpaper, the carefully framed glossy photos of show business personalities. Some of them were obviously publicity shots, posed in photographers' studios, autographed and passed out to promote the singers and actors and comedians of the past half century. Others showed celebrities posed with a smiling man in chef's garb. Well-dressed, carefully groomed men and women in the latest fashions of 1950, 1965, 1988, always young, always grinning, and the chef at first with black wavy hair and a pencil-line mustache, his hair growing lighter and his mustache heavier with the passing decades.

Lindsey said, 'Ducky R dropped this one on me without warning. I read the case folder on the plane but it's pretty skimpy. How much more do you know about it?'

'You know Mark Zilbert from Chi branch?'

'Never heard of him.' Lindsey shook his head.

'Decent guy. Run of the mill claims agent. Soon as he saw what was going on he ID'd this one for SPUDS.'

'The policy wasn't for megabucks.' Lindsey speared a mushroom and chewed it meditatively. 'Not a lot of dollars but apparently International Surety got itself into some kind of fiduciary relationship when the policy was issued in, when was it, 1944. It wasn't an I.S. policy back then, it was one of the precursor companies, but I.S. is responsible. And now we're supposed to return the claimant's property and it's nowhere to be found.'

'It's a little more complicated than that.' Gina speared a morsel of carpaccio, chewed and swallowed. 'There are a couple of oddities to this case. I'm kind of peeved with Ducky for not leaving it in my hands, but you're his fair-haired boy right now so I guess I'll just lean back and enjoy it.'

'Is that the weird part — the fiduciary arrangement?'

He watched Gina dip a cold boiled prawn into cocktail sauce.

Before taking a bite she said, 'That isn't the only oddity, but it's a big one.'

'Not the kind of thing we'd do today,

but I guess the company was struggling for business back then and they'd do whatever it took to get a policy written.'

Gina shrugged. Her shoulders, like the rest of her, were generously fleshed. In the hot Chicago summer a few drops of perspiration shimmered on her throat. She wore a black blouse of soft, shimmering material and a string of onyx beads.

'What else?' Lindsey asked.

'The claimant herself. You'll see.'

'The trouble with the case folder,' Lindsey resumed, 'there's less there than meets the eye. It doesn't even say what the property was, that I.S. was holding for the insured.'

The *maitre d'* had seated them and a crimson-jacketed waiter murmured that there was no need to order, he'd take care of them. The generous antipasto had arrived almost before they had time to unfold their white linen napkins. Now Gina's Uncle Aldo emerged from the kitchen in white jacket and tall chef's hat. He leaned over Gina and she planted a kiss on his cheek and said, '*Zio*, this is my associate, Bart Lindsey.'

'Sure. The only time I get to see my baby niece is when she brings people to eat.'

Lindsey stood halfway up, leaning across the table.

Uncle Aldo shook Lindsey's hand.

Lindsey said, 'How do you do, sir.'

Uncle Aldo nodded to Lindsey. 'Go on, children, I'm just gonna drink you in with my eyes.' Iron-gray curls peeked out beneath the edges of his chef's hat. His eyebrows and curved mustache were the same metallic color.

He slid into the banquette beside Gina. A third wine glass had appeared miraculously and been filled. Uncle Aldo raised the glass, studied the wine against the comfortable room's amber-tinted lighting, then sipped carefully.

Lindsey shot a glance at Gina. She smiled back, 'You can say anything in front of Uncle Aldo.'

A busboy cleared the remnants of the antipasto. Their waiter reappeared bearing platters of food. Uncle Aldo eyed the viands the way an infantry colonel would study a freshly cleaned and oiled rifle at white-glove inspection time.

'What I got from the folder,' Lindsey said, 'was that I.S. issued a tontine policy in 1944 to three young women.'

'Really just girls,' Gina said.

Lindsey looked at her sideways. 'How come you know so much about this case?'

'I was curious.'

'You read the file before it went to Denver?'

Gina grinned. She mopped the droplets of sweat from her chest with her linen napkin.

Lindsey snorted. 'Okay. Go on, then.' Before she could resume, he addressed Gina's uncle. 'Is this insurance matter boring you, sir? You don't have to sit through it.'

The old man made a palms-up gesture. 'It's late. No more customers. My people, they're closing up the kitchen now. You go ahead and eat and talk. Drink up your wine. That's good wine. I'll listen.'

'Sure.' Lindsey took a mouthful of the dry Italian vintage. 'You review the case for us, Gina, all right?'

Gina nodded. She was in no hurry,

though. She tore a piece of hard-crusted garlic toast in half, then tore a chunk from the half-slice, chewed it with a blissful expression and swallowed.

'Three little girls named Gloria in the same classroom. Right here at St. Cecelia's. You know the school, Bart?'

'I'm a California boy. I'm a visitor.'

'You could walk from here. On Laramie, down near the racetrack.' She tilted her head as if to point the way.

'She's-a gone,' Uncle Aldo said. His Italian accent grew heavier as he spoke of the past. He reached for the garlic toast and held it in both his hands, as tenderly as if it were a newborn child. He studied it, sniffed its aroma, tasted it carefully. 'Not the best garlic this year. I don't know what's-a the matter with the farmers.'

Lindsey asked, 'Who's gone?'

'Nobody's-a gone.'

'You said — '

'The school, they tore it down, they put up condos. Diocese got lots of money, people move in there, send their kids to private schools. No room for St. Cecelia's no more. No kids to go there either. Now

212

the condos, they're not doing so good neither. All a big waste.'

'I knew that,' Gina stated. 'I'm sorry. I was a CeCe girl myself, I can still see the school when I go by. Like a ghost.' She heaved a sigh. 'But this was more than fifty years ago, Uncle Aldo.'

'I know, I know,' the old man grumbled. He took over the story from his niece. 'These three Glorias, they all meet in first grade and they drive the sisters crazy. They get whacks on the knuckles with a ruler until their hands they bleed. They get sent to the principal's office, they got to say more Hail Marys than you can count, they get sent home with notes to their parents. Nothing stopped them.' He shook his head ruefully, as if the events of a half century before had taken place that day.

Lindsey listened and chewed.

Uncle Aldo took a sip of wine and nodded.

'Gloria Verdi, she always said she was related to Giuseppe Verdi, the great Verdi. Gloria Rossi, everybody says her family was Communists. And Gloria Dorato.'

'Meaning?' Lindsey waited.

213

Gina translated for Lindsey. 'Meaning, *golden*. Their names meant Gloria Green, Gloria Red, Gloria Gold. They always wore their theme colors and they always hung out together.'

'You knew them?' Lindsey asked.

'I was too young to know them,' Gina asserted. 'By the time I went to St. Cecelia's they were legends. They were famous by then. The sisters made them heroes by the time I went there.'

'I knew those girls,' Uncle Aldo put in. His voice was strong and steady. It matched his heavy-boned, powerful hands. It was not the voice of an old man, nor were his hands an old man's hands. 'Everybody in the neighborhood used to know each other. It's not like that no more.'

Lindsey's eyebrows rose. This was the kind of work he enjoyed. When you got away from headquarters and went out and talked to people you could often learn more in a few days than you could by punching paper for a month. 'What do you think, Uncle Aldo? Is it all right if I call you that?'

'You're Gina's friend,' Uncle Aldo

nodded, 'you have my permission.'

Somehow, Lindsey realized, it was a good thing that he had asked and not just used the name. He asked, 'When was that, Uncle Aldo? You remember what year that was?'

'I started St. Cecelia's 1932.' the old man said. 'I was six years old. The Glorias, they was three-four years ahead of me.' He smiled at the recollection, a faraway look in his faded gray eyes. 'Those girls, I remember those big girls, eh? They always wore hair ribbons. All the girls they wore hair ribbons in those days. They always wore their colors, those three. Green, red, gold. Everybody recognize them everyplace they go. Their families was poor, everybody was poor in those days. But everybody scraped up a few dollars for the school, they didn't want to send the children to the public school, they was afraid the children wouldn't know about God so they sent them to the nuns.'

Lindsey waited. The restaurant was empty now except for the three of them and the staff, cleaning up, closing up. Their crimson-jacketed waiter put dishes in front of Gina and Lindsey; a veal chop with greens, a thin, broad portion of golden sole, a side dish of pasta in red sauce for each. *Green, gold, red.* Uncle Aldo reached and sliced into Gina's chop, nodded his approval, tasted Lindsey's broiled fish, said, 'It's okay, you can eat.'

Gina shot a glance at Lindsey that said, without her speaking a word, *You see how I love my Zio Aldo.*

Lindsey said, 'The policy — whoever wrote it back in 1944, it's pretty weird. If it was just the cash we'd cut a check and be done with it in a minute. It's the fiduciary angle that has Desmond Richelieu riled up.'

The pasta was as delicate as a breeze; the red sauce held the tang and scent of unfamiliar herbs.

'What I don't understand,' Lindsey said, 'the claim isn't in the name of any of these Glorias. It says, uh, just a minute.' He flipped his pocket organizer open and punched a few keys. 'It says, Mary Joseph. She made her claim using the old policy number, but there's no Mary Joseph in the file. But that's the claimant's name, at this address, you see, right here in Cicero.'

The old man leaned over Lindsey's shoulder and peered at the electronic screen. He made a clucking sound with his tongue. 'That's where the school was. That's one of the condo buildings. When the school close, they make one of the buildings a home for the old nuns, the ones too old to take other work. It's their convent. St. Cecelia's Convent. They only had a little Order, they ran the school. Now they're dying out. No new sisters. There's hardly any left. Once they're gone — ' He made a gesture with his hands, palms upward, as if he were freeing captive birds, sending them into the sky. 'We send them dinners, *grazie*, for the old nuns.'

Now Lindsey was puzzled. 'I thought the three Glorias were students at St. Cecelia's.'

Aldo nodded. 'Yes, yes. But later, one Gloria, she comes back and take her vows. The others, oh, one was a nurse, she was killed in Korea, it was terrible. She never wanted nothing for herself, she just wanted to help people. Such a young woman, such a shame. She got sent over there.' He grimaced, ran a gnarled hand over his face and nodded agreement to some invisible presence.

'The other one, she died too. She was in show business, a big success, a lot of husbands.' He shook his head and crossed himself as if the sin of multiple marriages might rub off on him. 'She gets sick, the doctors try and help her but they say she got lung cancer. They cut her up, they shoot the rays in her, it don't do no good for her and she dies.'

He paused. The sound of a vacuum cleaner came to Lindsey's ears as a worker ran an industrial grade machine across the restaurant's heavy carpeting. 'She used to smoke them cigarettes all the time, them Mountainaire Menthols they call them. That's how she got that cancer.'

He paused again, and the only sound in the room was the hum of the vacuum cleaner engine. 'But one of them,' Aldo resumed, 'one of them is still alive. One Gloria. She's a nun. She was a teacher, now she's retired. She lives where the old school was.'

Lindsey asked which of the Glorias had

survived. 'Dorato. Gloria Verdi, she was the nurse. Gloria Rossi, she was the showgirl. Beautiful. Sang, danced, everything. At first everybody was proud of our Gloria, the neighborhood, but then she went to California, she got married, divorced, married, divorced.' He shook his head sadly.

'Wait, you come with me.' Aldo rose from the banquette and reached back to wrap his massive fingers around Lindsey's wrist. He lifted him from his seat as if he were a child. He led him across the now-vacant dining room, Lindsey casting a fleeting, half-panicked glance at Gina Rossellini who rose to her feet and followed the two men.

Aldo halted in front of a framed black-and-white photo. For a moment Lindsey failed to recognize him. It showed Aldo as a young man. It was the only photo in the room that showed him without a mustache, but the smile was the same as in the other photos. He wore a World War II era Marine Corps uniform. Lindsey could make out a sergeant's chevrons on Aldo's uniform sleeve and a row of campaign ribbons on his chest.

Lindsey felt a presence behind him, felt a warm pressure on his back, smelled Gina Rossellini's perfume, felt her warm breath on the back of his neck.

'That's when I come back from the Pacific,' Aldo said. 'That's the Glory Girls. You see?' He still held Lindsey's wrist in his powerful grasp. With the other hand he pointed to the figures in the photo. 'You see, that's Verdi, that's Rossi, that's Dorato. She's dead. She's dead. But she's alive. She's still alive.'

At their table again Gina sipped espresso; Aldo, a glowing yellow, syrupy Galliano; Lindsey, cappuccino. They picked at biscotti. Lindsey said, 'Uncle Aldo, tell me again which Gloria was which.'

'Verdi was the nurse,' the old man said, 'Rossi was the showgirl, Dorato is the nun.'

As they left the restaurant Gina embraced the old man. '*Zio mio.*'

'*Cara nipote.*'

She drove Lindsey to a Travelodge in Berwyn. They sat in the lobby making plans. Lindsey said that he wanted to visit Mary Joseph in the morning, find out what he could about the claim. Rossellini offered to accompany him. He didn't know the streets, didn't really know his way around this town at all. He was happy to accept.

★   ★   ★

He sat up in bed with the case folder in his lap, going over the paperwork still again. The members of the tontine were the three Glorias, but the claimant was identified as Mary Joseph. It didn't take a Stephen Hawking to figure out that Mary Joseph was Gloria Dorato, Gloria Dorato after she had become a nun with a new name.

If she still lived at the old nuns' condo on Laramie Avenue, on the site of the onetime St. Cecelia's school, a brief visit should settle matters. Lindsey would be on his way back to Denver by nightfall. That was, if he could settle the mystery of the fiduciary trust. What had International Surety's predecessor company taken in trust for the three Glory Girls half a century ago? What was it, where was it, and why was it valuable?

If not for that puzzle, Gina Rossellini could surely have handled the case herself. For that matter, Mark Zilbert could have done it, there would have been no need to call in SPUDS at all.

If Gloria Dorato had become Mary Joseph, then Mary Joseph would give him the answer to the puzzle, the key to the treasure chest. He would retrieve the treasure for her, the sister would be happy, International Surety would have done its duty, Lindsey would be a hero, the case would be closed.

He closed the case folder and slipped it into his attaché case. He clicked the remote to the weather forecast, hoping for relief from the heat. Instead he saw footage of tornadoes tearing up farms in Indiana followed by a report of waterspouts and thunderstorms over Lake Michigan. He switched to an all-night movie station and watched Lloyd Nolan as Michael Shayne save the otherwise forgotten Margery Weaver from her dangerous addiction to gambling. He made it to the end of the picture, clicked the set and the room into darkness and closed his eyes.

★ ★ ★

The next morning Lindsey found Gina Rossellini waiting for him in the air-conditioned lobby of the Travelodge. When they stepped into the street they were hit by a blast of heat that staggered Lindsey. He found Rossellini's fingers on his elbow; they felt as powerful as her Uncle Aldo's had the night before.

She said, 'You want to get breakfast?'

They took a light meal, then climbed into Rossellini's Viper. She drove through sweltering streets, then pulled into the courtyard of a complex of buff-colored low-rise apartments on Laramie Avenue. One building was marked with a crucifix above its portico.

Lindsey felt uncomfortable. He was uncertain about what to expect. 'I've never been in a convent,' he told Rossellini. 'I thought they didn't let men inside.'

Rossellini said, 'I went to St. Cecelia's, Bart, so the sisters know me. Don't let them scare you.'

He stood back while she rang the doorbell. After a long wait the door was opened to reveal a gray-haired woman in a plain dress of pale linen. She wore a crucifix on a beaded chain. It looked heavy, as if its weight might make her topple over. Her face and body were thin. Her eyes were so faded that they matched her colorless dress.

She looked up at Rossellini and after a moment she smiled. 'Gina.' They embraced, the heavy-boned and fleshy Rossellini and the tiny, fragile nun.

Rossellini said, 'Sister, this is Mr. Lindsey. From International Surety. He's here about the tontine.' To Lindsey she said, 'This is Sister Michael Judith, Mother Superior of the Convent.'

The old nun extended her hand and Lindsey took it. Her skin was like dry silk; through it he could feel her bones, as light as a pet avian's.

She said, 'Come in. Would you like something cold? We have iced tea.'

Lindsey and Rossellini declined the offer.

Sister Michael Judith led them to a small parlor. It was furnished with a couch, chairs and coffee table that would have been turned down by any second-rate motel. The room was decorated with a large crucifix and some cheap religious prints. A tall clock stood in one corner, its pendulum swinging behind an etched glass panel.

Lindsey laid his attaché case on the coffee table. He sat in a faded armchair. Gina Rossellini and Sister Michael Judith sat on the spindly-legged couch. Lindsey opened the attaché case and took out the red-covered case folder. He said, 'We have an old policy here, uh, should I call you Miss Judith or — ?'

The old woman smiled. 'You're not Catholic, Mr. Lindsey.'

'No.'

'Well, Sister would be fine. Just Sister. But if you're uneasy with that — '

'No, ah, that's, ah, Sister.' He turned the folder around and laid it down again. 'The policy was drawn in 1944 to Gloria Verdi, Gloria Rossi, and Gloria Dorato. Whichever of the three co-holders should survive, will collect a cash payment and receive certain fiduciary holdings. The policy was paid in full by 1974, thirty years of premiums. Now International Surety is ready to issue the payment, but we have two small problems.'

He heard himself say that, say *small problems*. That was partly true. Problems, yes. Small, maybe not.

As the two women sat side by side, Sister Michael Judith's hand lay in Gina Rossellini's. They looked like a mother and child, Rossellini the mother holding her child's thin, small hand, ready to do anything it took to protect her from the world.

'Yes, Mr. Lindsey,' the old nun asked, 'two problems.'

'The first,' Lindsey cleared his throat, 'ah, the first is Mary Joseph.'

'Sister Mary Joseph.'

'Yes. I understand, ah, from Miss Rossellini's Uncle Aldo, that Gloria Dorato is Sister Mary Joseph. Is that correct?'

'Yes.'

'Is she here? May I speak with her? Can this be verified?'

'Yes,' Sister Michael Judith said, 'and yes, and yes. But will she speak with you?' She smiled again, but sadly. 'Sometimes she is here with us, sometimes she seems to be in another place. Or in another time. Do you understand what I mean, Mr. Lindsey?'

Lindsey did. His own mother had wandered for years, half-dazed, one day a bride in 1952, the next a widow in another year, the next somewhere else in time, burying herself in decades-old picture magazines and watching black-and-white motion pictures, fleeing in terror and revulsion from the modern world.

'I understand, Sister.'

'I'm afraid we don't have papers,' the nun said. 'When we lost the old school — everything was in the school, you see. The diocese was supposed to take charge of our records but something went wrong, somebody, what's the expression, somebody just didn't get the word. We lost everything. Everything.'

She managed a faint, wistful smile. 'Nothing is certain save for death and taxes, isn't that so? Even salvation — we believe in salvation, Mr. Lindsey, but even the strongest faith falters at times, I must admit.'

She heaved a sigh that Lindsey feared would crack her fragile ribs but she closed her free hand around the crucifix on her chest, drawing strength from it. 'This building has not been a great success.' Lindsey wondered why she had changed the subject. 'If we had some money,' she said, 'I know we could buy the building from the landlord. I've discussed it with him. We could open our school again. There aren't many of us left and I don't know if we could attract new sisters. Maybe we could get lay teachers. I'm afraid our Order is dying. When we lost our purpose we lost our will to live, don't you see? Our Order is like a living thing, and now that it has no purpose in life it's dying.'

She used both hands, now, to hold onto Gina Rossellini's hand. The nun's two hands, together, were smaller than Rossellini's one.

'If only we had the papers to prove that Sister Mary Joseph is Gloria Dorato, your company would pay us some money. I was hoping we could buy the building from the landlord and we would get our school back. But you see, we have no papers.'

Lindsey said, 'Maybe we can work that out. I can't promise, but I think we can swing it. But I'm afraid there won't be enough money coming to her — will she turn the money over to your Order, Sister? Is that how it works?'

'Yes, that is how it works.'

'Well, it still won't amount to much. But the fiduciary — ' He paused. The room was filled by the ticking of the tall clock.

'You've mentioned that. I'm sorry, I just don't understand things like that. The diocese always took care of things like that, but I guess they have greater problems to occupy their minds. Now — I just don't know.'

'That's the other problem, Sister. I don't know what the trust is.' He held up the red folder. 'It's referred to in the file but it isn't described, not what it is nor where it is.'

The old nun smiled once again.

'Maybe if we asked Sister Mary Joseph,' Rossellini suggested.

The old nun beside her rose carefully to her feet, working her hands up

Rossellini's arm like a cat climbing a tree. 'Wait here, please. I'll bring her if I can.'

Before she moved away from him and Rossellini, Lindsey asked, 'Would it be all right if I record our conversation?' He lifted a miniature DAT recorder from his attaché case.

Sister Michal Judith gazed at the machine, as much bafflement filling her face as if he'd laid a miniature nuclear reactor on the coffee table. 'I don't know if Sister Mary Joseph will quite understand — whether she can truly give her consent. But I suppose — I don't see any harm in it, if it doesn't upset her.' She stood for half a minute, breathing slowly, gathering her strength, and walked with great care from the room.

Rossellini locked eyes with Lindsey. The tall clock ticked. Speaking softly, Lindsey asked Rossellini if she knew Gloria Dorato, Sister Mary Joseph. She nodded. He asked if he knew the cause of her condition. Softly, she said, 'Alzheimer's.' It was a word whispered the way *cancer* once had been whispered.

Sister Michael Judith returned, leading

another woman. She was similarly dressed. She was not as thin, not as frail in appearance, but her expression was vacant. Gina Rossellini slid to the end of the couch to make room for the new arrival. Sister Michael Judith guided her to a place on the couch, pressed her shoulder until she sat down, then joined her.

'Mr. Lindsey, this is Sister Mary Joseph. She used to be Gloria Dorato.'

Lindsey held his hand toward the woman. When she didn't respond he started to draw back but Sister Michael Judith sent him a look of encouragement and he took the newcomer's hand in both of his, held it briefly, then released it.

An expression flitted across Sister Mary Joseph's face. Lindsey was unable to read it, but at least it was a reaction.

'Sister,' he said, 'do you remember when you were Gloria Dorato? Do you remember Gloria Verdi and Gloria Rossi?'

She looked at him, confused.

'You went to school together. Do you remember?'

She opened her mouth, then shut it again, a surprised expression in her eyes.

She shook her head, opened and shut her mouth once more as if she hadn't done that in decades, maybe ever, and was just learning or relearning how to do it.

She said, 'The Glory Girls. We were the Glory Girls.'

Sister Michael Judith reached and smoothed Sister Mary Joseph's hair.

Gina Rossellini stared.

Lindsey said, 'Tell me about the Glory Girls.'

Sister Mary Joseph raised her hands to shoulder height and began to sing in a dry, tiny voice. Her voice grew stronger as she sang.

We're red, we're gold, we're green,
We're too good to be seen,
When justice calls us then you know,
We're right here on your radio.

She put her hands to her face and squeezed her eyes shut. She repeated the last line, drawing out the words as if she wanted them to go on forever. 'We're right here on your ray-de-oh-oh-oh-oh-oh.' With her eyes still shut she said, 'We have an insurance policy. I know the number. I remember the number.' She recited it. It was correct, to the digit.

She opened her eyes and turned to Sister Michael Judith. 'Take me to my room. Please take me to my room.' She appeared to be on the verge of tears, but before they could come her face relaxed, returned to its blankness. Then her eyes focused again and she said to Lindsey, 'Are you coming to the dance? Don't you have to report back to base, young man? I know there's a war on but our girls are good girls. Every one of them is a good girl.'

The light faded from her face. She breathed softly and steadily.

Sister Michael Judith struggled to her feet. Drawing upon some supernatural reservoir of strength, she lifted Sister Mary Joseph and led her from the room.

Rossellini said, 'Bart, I can swear to it. She's Gloria Dorato. I'm positive. I.S. can make out that check any time. God knows the sisters need it.'

When Sister Michael Judith returned, Lindsey and Rossellini were both on their feet. Lindsey said, 'Thank you, Sister. I didn't mean to upset her.'

Sister Michal Judith extended her weightless hand again. 'I should thank you, Mr. Lindsey. This was the first time in weeks that she's shown any interest in anything. You're leaving now?'

'I'll try to get that check to you.'

'Please.'

'You're sure you have no documents? No fingerprints, medical records?'

'All gone. Everything is gone.' She walked them to the door.

His hand on the doorknob, Lindsey turned back once more. 'Sister, may I ask, how many of you there are?'

'Just the two of us,' she told him.

The sun was beating down on the courtyard and when Rossellini opened the driver's door in the Viper a blast of torrid air exploded from the car. She slid into the driver's seat and turned on the air conditioner. She stood with Lindsey while the car blew out its store of heat and moisture.

'Any ideas?' Lindsey asked her.

'Glory Girls on the radio. 'We're right

here on your ray-dee-oh-oh-oh,'' she mimicked. 'Sounds like your favorite kind of case to me.'

'I guess I'm saddled with that rep. We could try the library. Or — let's find a yellow pages and see if there's a dealer who handles vintage broadcast materials. I never heard of the Glory Girls, but 1944 was before my time.'

'Mine too!' Rossellini delivered her response with more force than Lindsey would have expected.

'I didn't mean to imply otherwise.'

'Okay.'

They found a classified at a phone booth and settled on an establishment called Wavelength Heaven on Maxwell near Jefferson. Rossellini drove them there and parked the Viper in a commercial garage.

Wavelength Heaven was in heaven, all right. Up two flights of rickety stairs above a barber shop, an old-fashioned non-franchise hamburger joint called Minnie's, and a floor of office suites so old they had wooden doors with pebbled-glass panels and the names of long-departed tenants still visible in flaking gilt.

The stairwell offered protection from the searing sunlight but the air in it was musty and painfully hot to the lungs.

Someone had taped a computer-printed sign to one glass panel, identifying the establishment that lay behind it as Wavelength Heaven. Lindsey held his attaché case in one hand and raised the other to knock on the door but before knuckles met glass an angry shout froze him in his tracks. The reply was cut off by a booming explosion, the frantic pounding of running feet, a slamming door, the roar of an engine keyed to life and the screech of tires pulling away from a curb.

Lindsey and Rossellini exchanged shocked looks.

The shout came again, the interrupted reply, the booming explosion — it could be the discharge of a heavy-caliber pistol, more likely a shotgun — the running feet . . .

Lindsey rapped sharply on the glass.

The sounds continued briefly, their volume diminishing.

Lindsey pounded his fist on the door.

The sounds stopped. The door opened

a few inches and a woman said, 'All right, I'll use the phones, you don't have to — oh!' The door opened farther, revealing a striking figure. She was close to six feet tall, with skin the color of mahogany and the texture of satin and frizzed jet black hair. In the stifling weather she wore a black tank top with a white band at the chest, black leotards, and dazzling white running shoes.

'I thought you were the bucket-shop bozo,' she said. 'What can I do for you?'

Lindsey showed her his International Surety ID and introduced himself and Gina Rossellini. 'I'm processing an insurance claim and I hoped you might give me, us, some help.'

The tall woman grinned. Her teeth were as white as her sneakers. 'Insurance claim. How many times have I heard that one!'

'No, really.' Lindsey shook his head. 'You can check with my company. Our company. Miss Rossellini is from the Chicago office, or my own office in Denver — '

'Denver, hey? If this is a scam you're in

the wrong establishment, but at least it sounds interesting. Come in. Wait a minute while I shut this thing down.' She hit some controls on an oversized tape deck. 'Trying to clean this thing up, nobody has an ET and this tape must be a zillionth generation.'

Rossellini put in, 'ET? As in the movie?'

'ET, as in electrical transcription. They're the best source for a lot of classic radio shows, but most of them were destroyed decades ago.'

Lindsey said, 'This is Wavelength Heaven?'

'Wendy Wavelength, in person.' She picked a pair of business cards from a holder in the counter and extended them to Lindsey and Rossellini. They returned the favor.

'What a name!'

'Well, I teach stress analysis and some other physics tracks at U Chi as Gwen Weiner. The Wendy Wavelength name was a joke at first, but once my business started to take off I was kind of stuck with it. But it's fun.'

Gina Rossellini was standing with her head cocked to one side. She said, 'Keep talking.' When Wendy spoke again Gina squeezed her eyes shut.

Wendy said, 'Okay, sure, I've been through this before, I know the drill, I figure it's coming right about — *now!*'

'I know you!' Gina opened her eyes and straightened her head. 'I used to hear you all the time. You were on WLDY. I used to hear you late at night.'

'You got me.' Wendy grinned. '*Wavelength Heaven* used to be my show. That's how the business got started. People kept calling up, writing me letters, asking about old shows. So I finally started the company. Then we got a new manager at the station and — '

'I know,' Rossellini took over, 'All oldies, all the time, nothing but good, grand, great old oldies!'

'Meaning, nothing older than doo-wop and guaranteed two Buddy Holly tracks and a Sam Cooke every hour. Not that I have anything against Buddy or Sam or the doo-woppers but, good grief, the world wasn't created during Ike's second term. But you couldn't prove it by Mister Pinstriped Suit Milton Jeckler. Isn't that a perfect name, Milton Jeckler? They sent him down from network HQ, Falcon-Eagle Network, good old right-wing ranter FEN, to turn WLDY into all oldies, all the time.'

It looked to Lindsey as if Gina and Wendy were discovering they were best friends. 'Maybe we could tend to our business.'

'Sorry.' Wendy made an odd, ocean-wave movement with one long-fingered hand. 'Did you want to buy some tapes? This is mainly a catalog operation, you know.' She produced what looked like a colorful magazine; on the cover was a picture of a woman in 40's drag and an upswept hairdo emoting into a micro-phone. Wendy handed copies to each of them.

'But as long as you're here, if you want to buy some tapes or some other merchan-dise, that's all right with me.'

'Actually we were just after some information.' Lindsey slipped the glossy catalog into his attaché case.

Wendy Wavelength frowned. 'If this were a hobby-oriented visit, I'd be happy to chat with you for a while, then I have to get back to work. The semester ended and now's my chance to catch up on the radio side. But if we're doing business you'll have to cross my palm with silver.'

'We can do that,' Lindsey nodded. 'What's your hourly rate for consulting?'

She named a figure.

He said, 'Raise your right hand. By the power invested in me by the Special Projects Unit, Detached Status, I hereby dub thee Special Consultant to International Surety Corporation.'

Gwen Weiner looked baffled, then burst into laughter. She shook Lindsey's hand, swung a muscular arm around his shoulders and said, 'Come into my executive suite.' She moved around them, locking the door with its pebbled-glass panel, then led the way past the counter and an array of electronic gear. Behind a bank of dials and blinking lights that would have done a sci-fi movie proud was an alcove with half a dozen battered chairs and a scratched and stained table.

Gina Rossellini went head-to-head with Lindsey. 'You've certainly got frisky since the last time we worked together.'

He said, 'I guess I've learned a few things.'

'I'll say you have.'

Gwen Weiner gestured around the alcove. 'A little group of radio hobbyists — we get together here for bull-sessions.' She waited while Lindsey and Rossellini settled into a couple of ancient easy chairs, then asked, 'What are you looking for, Mr. Lindsey?'

Lindsey explained International Surety's obligation to Gloria Dorato *aka* Sister Mary Joseph. 'Assuming that we can establish that Sister Mary Joseph really is Gloria Dorato. If we can solve that one, then Ms. Rossellini and I have to track down the — whatever it is.'

'McGuffin,' said Gwen Weiner.

'Pardon?'

'The McGuffin. Surely you know your Hitchcock.'

'Sorry,' Lindsey smiled. 'Of course. The Maltese Falcon. The Bruce-Partington Plans.'

'The thing in the box,' Gwen Weiner

supplied. 'It could be anything, could even be nothing. It's the thing that everybody wants, that makes the story work.'

'Touché.'

'And you say this Gloria Dorato was one of the Glory Girls. What I wouldn't give for some Glory Girls shows to sell through Wavelength Heaven.'

Lindsey said, 'I never heard of that show.'

'I'm not surprised. Ms. Rossellini, you say you knew my program.'

'I did. I loved some of the old stories you played. *Inner Sanctum. Wendy Warren with the News. Nightbeat.* But I don't remember *Glory Girls.*'

'No surprise there. I don't have any *Glory Girls* shows. Nobody does. The program was produced right here in Chicago, on the old WING. You wouldn't remember that either. 'Let your imagination take wing with WING.' Before our time, sister. They did a lot of great shows there, almost as many as WXYZ in Detroit or WOR in New York. But they changed format, changed call-letters, station was sold a couple of times, switched network affiliations, went indie, went network again. Nowadays

WLDY has WING's old license and they have their archives stashed somewhere in a warehouse. I've always had a sneaking suspicion there were some *Glory Girls* ET's in the WING archives, but wonderful Milton Jeckler wouldn't let me in there, won't even talk about it. Then, of course, with the new all-oldies format I got canned and the issue became moot. Besides, my plate is full enough between teaching my classes and running my business.'

Lindsey recognized a special gleam in Gina Rossellini's eyes. She said, 'Bart, Gwen — I'd have to check with Chicago branch, but I think I.S. wrote a commercial liability policy for Falcon-Eagle. They're part of a global conglomerate, and one of our corporate super-sellers landed their liability account.'

Gwen Weiner said, 'So what?'

Gina Rossellini said, 'So, if we're liable for damages they might cause, it's standard practice to drop in and check out hazards. Policy gives I.S. the right to do that.'

'You can do that on your own?'

'I think we'd better get some clearance from on high.'

'Not to worry.' Lindsey felt the blood pumping, the adrenaline flowing. 'One cellular to Ducky and we're on the move.'

Gwen Weiner looked crestfallen. 'You're on the move, maybe, but I'm the one who really wants to get in there, and I don't work for your company.'

Lindsey grinned. 'Sure you do. Your short-term memory failing already at your young age? You're an I.S. consultant.'

'Even so.' The crestfallen look gave way to one of worry. 'I don't even know where the warehouse is. I don't think anybody at the station does. Jeckler likes to play his hand really close to his chest. Anything he knows that nobody else knows — you see what I mean?'

'Hey, if International Surety holds the policy, the address is sure to be in our files.' Lindsey excused himself and placed a call to Desmond Richelieu in Denver.

* * *

The trick, Lindsey knew, was to bully or wheedle Jeckler into letting them into the warehouse without letting him know what they were really after — or how important it might be. Lindsey had got Richelieu's approval for the operation with minimal trouble. When he'd first been assigned to SPUDS it looked like the kiss of death to his career in International Surety, but when he turned one headline case after another to the advantage and often to the good reputation of the company, he had won Richelieu's first grudging, then enthusiastic, support.

Richelieu told Lindsey that he'd have Mrs. Blomquist prepare a fancy document at once. Richelieu would sign it and have it notarized and express-delivered to Lindsey overnight.

That night Lindsey and Gina Rossellini shared a late meal at a seafood house near the Loop, then found a bistro where they lingered over liqueurs and listened to a torch singer who must have spent her life studying Billie Holiday and Sarah Vaughn and working to amalgamate their phrasing into her own lighter voice. Between sets Gina told Lindsey about her childhood in Chicago, her parents and sisters and her *Zio* Aldo and her *Zia* Giuseppina,

Aldo's long-dead wife.

She drove back to the Travelodge and pulled into a parking slot. 'We'll need to get over to Chicago branch in the morning to pick up your letters of marque,' she told Lindsey.

'Is it a long drive home for you?' he asked. 'The company would certainly spring for a cab.'

'I always keep an emergency overnight kit in the Viper,' she said.

★　★　★

Gwen Weiner met them at Wavelength Heaven the next day, by appointment. She had abandoned her tank top and leotards for a baggy white shirt and tight blue jeans. She wore the same sneakers as the previous day, or an identical pair.

Lindsey had his authorization from Desmond Richelieu in hand. He phoned WLDY and had a hard time reaching Milton Jeckler until he mentioned the magic phrase *liability insurance*. Yes, that would rattle Milton's cage all right.

He played it low-key, asked for an

appointment. Yes, it was urgent but no, there was nothing to worry about, but yes, it was a somewhat sensitive matter. Jeckler invited him to come over.

He faced Jeckler across the station manager's huge glass-topped desk and explained that International Surety had been troubled by a series of dubious policies and bogus claims. SPUDS was the company's own little internal affairs division and it was Lindsey's job to make sure that everything was kosher with as important an account as Falcon-Eagle.

Of course, here was Lindsey's identification and here was his authorization from Denver. Of course, Jeckler was free to contact Desmond Ricihelieu and check Lindsey out, he'd be happy to have Jeckler do so.

But if something fishy was going on in International Surety's Chicago office . . . What, corruption in *Chicago* of all places, who could even imagine such a thing? But if something fishy *was* going on in the Chicago office, International Surety would happily pay a major cash award to the party who helped them uncover it.

And International Surety was concerned that something not-quite-right was going on at the old WING warehouse.

WING? That was a joke! The old, so-called WING archives were nothing but a pile of ancient junk.

Still, if Lindsey could just take a look . . . Lindsey, assisted by a couple of colleagues . . . Milton Jeckler would personally accompany them.

No, that was a bad idea. Might smack of collusion. If Jeckler would simply authorize them to enter the warehouse . . .

That elicited a frown.

And if he would pledge solemnly not to warn the warehouse personnel that Lindsey and his crew were coming . . .

Milton Jeckler closed his eyes, screwed up his face, took a deep breath and held it until he started to redden. Finally the breath exploded from his nostrils, his eyes popped open and he whispered, 'All right. Go for it. You'll report back to me promptly? Terrific. And — good hunting!'

Lindsey managed to get out of WLDY without cracking a giant grin, no less dancing a celebratory jig.

He connected up with Rossellini and Weiner and they climbed into Rossellini's Viper. 'I guess you could have met Jeckler,' Lindsey told Gina, 'but I figured him for a man-to-man, just-us-guys type.'

'You got it right,' Weiner told him. 'I should have told you yesterday, when he fired me, it was because of the format change — officially. You'd never guess that he made a pretty crude pass at me and I tried out my judo on the creep.'

Gina snorted. 'Did it work?'

'Did Callas sing soprano?'

Weiner peered out the Viper's window, toward the lake. Lindsey asked if she had heard the weather forecast and she said that she had. He asked if she saw any sign of rain. She said, 'No, but I smell it.'

Gina Rossellini threaded a path between a limo as long as a locomotive and a towering SUV crammed with camping equipment and fishing gear with out-of-state license plates. Lindsey held his breath. Weiner hummed and nodded her approval.

They stopped for a late lunch, then headed for the warehouse. It was located on Lake Avenue in Mundelein, and it looked as if nobody used it for much of anything. Windows had been broken out and replaced with corrugated cardboard. A painted sign atop the building had long since faded to unreadability. There was wire mesh fence, however, with a wooden semblance of a guard-shack at the gate.

The guard wore a uniform cap. A matching jacket hung on a hook. A tarnished metallic badge above the uniform pocket read *Longinus*. The guard wore a sweat-stained black tee shirt with a life-size skull on the chest, a dagger through one eye-socket, blood dripping from the blade. A broken-toothed rat sat on the hilt, glaring at the world.

The guard himself was reading a comic book, moving his lips, picking at an acne-scab with his free hand.

Lindsey showed him his letter of authorization and said, 'We need to check the WING archive.'

'Never heard of it.'

'WLDY now.'

'Oh, yeah. I know them.'

'Please let us in.'

The guard thought about that for a very long time. He cast a needful glance at his telephone, abandoned his acne and moved his hand toward the receiver, then drew it back. 'Lemme see that letter again?'

Lindsey handed it to him.

When the kid handed it back he left perspiration fingerprints on it.

'Don't work for no International company. WLDY pays the security company and they pay me.'

'That's all right,' Lindsey told him, 'phone WLDY and ask for Mr. Jeckler.'

The kid looked blank. 'Who's Mr. Jeckler?'

'He's the big boss there,' Lindsey explained.

The kid looked at the telephone again, actually leaned toward it, then drew back once more and said, 'I guess it will be okay. But I can't show you around. I got to stay here and keep unauthorized people out.'

After a lengthy silence he rose slowly to his feet and lifted a key off a nail and handed it to Lindsey.

Gina Rossellini drove the Viper to the

entrance of the warehouse. As they climbed out of the car Gina Rossellini said, 'Did you catch that kid's name?'

Gwen Weiner said, 'Longinus. What kind of name is that, his mama call him after a wristwatch? And did you see that he was packing a revolver? My lord, it looked big enough to shoot down a bomber. What the heck is anybody thinking nowadays?'

Gina Rossellini said, 'Longinus was the Roman soldier who thrust his spear into Our Lord's wound.'

Gwen frowned. 'Let's just hope he doesn't get any ideas about thrusting that gun of his around. Incredible!'

They stood outside the warehouse for a few seconds while Lindsey fumbled the key into the old lock. It looked as if the lock had been undisturbed for months, maybe for years. During those few seconds he thought he heard the boom of distant thunder.

Inside the warehouse the electricity was still turned on. They found that out when they hit the row of switches beside the main door. Fully half the fluorescent bulbs in the ancient ceiling-hung fixtures were dead, and the others crackled and blinked, but they gave off enough light to work by.

Rows of dust-covered file cabinets.

Gwen Weiner pulled open a drawer and lifted a file folder. She spread it on a flat surface while Lindsey and Rossellini watched. She closed the folder, pulled another drawer open, removed a file, seemingly at random, laid it beside the first and made a humming sound somewhere deep in her chest.

Minutes later she turned to the others, grinning, her face and white shirt smudged with dust. 'This place is full of scripts. I guess we ought to check everything they have here but I don't see any business records, they must have shipped those out to FEN when WING became WLDY and they dumped everything they had. But they have all these classic era scripts, stuff from the 30's and 40's and 50's, stuff I never even imagined they'd saved.'

She whirled like a ballerina. 'I'm loose in Santa's workshop. They have all of it here. *Mr. Mystery Meets Murder, The Haunted Hour, Nick Train-Spycatcher, Hall of Heart's Desire, Wanda the Wizard, Six-Shooter Simmons, Glory Girls* — '

'Wait a minute. They have *Glory Girls* scripts?'

Gwen Weiner danced to a dark wooden file cabinet and opened a drawer. 'I saved the best for last. They have everything. April '44 to June '47. And look!' She pulled a folder, spread its contents on a table. 'All this promotional material. They had a Junior Glory Girls Club, here's a sample membership certificate and membership card, here's a Junior Glory Girls *Bulletin*. Look at the picture on the cover!'

Lindsey and Rossellini leaned in, one on either side of Gwen.

The magazine featured a drawing of three young women in colorful costumes. They looked like a cross between circus acrobats and superheroes. The capes, tights and boots were of matching patterns, one red, one green, one gold. Each Glory Girl wore a Glory Girls symbol on her chest.

Was it possible, Lindsey wondered, that the vibrant teenager Golden Glory had turned into the lost, wizened Sister Mary Joseph?

He knew that it was.

A brilliant flash illuminated the warehouse. The fluorescent lights flickered, then returned to their sputtering task. Heavy raindrops and what might even have been hailstones rattled off the galvanized iron roof and grimed windows like a barrage of shotgun pellets.

'What are those scripts worth, Gwen?' This was something Lindsey had to know.

'They're collectible, but mostly they go to universities. We might find a publisher willing to do a book of them, but that would be a specialty house. They pay peanuts. If only they'd saved their ET's.'

'I don't know that we ought to hang around here too long,' Rossellini put in. 'I think we're maybe pushing our luck already.'

Lindsey said, 'Longinus there is probably snuggled in his guard shack. He wouldn't want to get wet. Still, I think you're right.'

'One more try,' Weiner pleaded. Before Lindsey or Rossellini could react she disappeared between rows of storage racks. Then came something between a scream and a yelp. She might have come face to face with a leering maniac — or with Santa in person.

Her voice echoed back to them over the rattling rain and hail. 'They're here! Everything is here!'

Lindsey and Rossellini scurried after the sound of her voice. They found her standing in front of a ceiling-high rack stacked with flat corrugated-cardboard boxes. It looked like the storage room of a pizza restaurant.

Gwen Weiner was clutching a box to her chest. 'Look at the label. *Glory Girls* test show, February '44. WING, Chicago. Sponsor: Mountainaire Menthol Cigarettes. And look.' She swung her free hand up. 'Look at the dates, this has to be a complete run of the show. And they have everything here. All the others. They were syndicating the WING shows and they kept a master set of ETs here and nobody knows about it, nobody even remembers.'

She caught Lindsey's eye and didn't wait for him to ask the question. 'These are worth serious money. Not the disks themselves, there are a few collectors who go for transcription disks, but we can dub cassettes and CD's from these, it's a growing market, Wavelength Heaven can really soar.'

Rossellini said, 'We'd better clear out. It's getting dark.'

Lindsey trotted a few yards to a place where he could see the windows. The rain had washed away some of the grime but the natural light was fading fast.

'Longinus is probably going off shift about now,' Rossellini continued. 'We'll have to deal with the night guy. He might even have a brain. That would make him more dangerous.'

Lindsey said, 'Okay. I'll have to consult my boss again before we do anything. Gwen, you'll have to put everything back as we found it.'

'Oh, no.' She shook her head. 'Oh, no. You don't know Milton Jeckler the way I do. You don't know his bosses at Falcon-Eagle. Once they get word they'll seal this place up like Fort Knox.' She paused. 'Or they'll have a fire. Your company would love that, wouldn't it, Mr. Lindsey? What's this place insured for?'

'You're right. We'll have to act fast, before Jeckler catches on. Tell you what. Damn, this isn't easy. All right. Gwen, you take the most important disk. Just one.'

'That's easy. This one. *Glory Girls* inaugural show, it's even more important than their audition show.'

'And some scripts.'

She selected half a dozen and Lindsey crammed them into his attaché case.

They climbed back into the Viper and headed back to the guard shack. Longinus was gone, replaced by his twin sister, Drusilla. Drusilla studied Lindsey's credentials as if she could actually read and waved them through the gates, back onto the rain-drenched street. The rain had let up and the superheated pavement was turning the freshly fallen water into vapor, sending it back into the atmosphere as if the whole city had become a massive steam-bath.

Gwen Weiner asked to be dropped at her shop. 'I want to transfer this disk before anything can happen to it. I want to get it into my computer.'

Gina Rossellini headed back toward Maxwell. A few blocks before they reached Wavelength Heaven she pulled the Viper to the curb and climbed out. They picked up a pizza and an iced six-pack and drove the rest of the way.

Gwen Weiner carried the transcription disk up the flights of stairs as if it were the Holy Grail. In her workshop she opened the carton and laid the disk on a turntable while Gina Rossellini opened the pizza carton and set about slicing the steaming pie.

The rainstorm had passed over Chicago and the temperature had dropped precipitously. It might be possible to eat the hot pizza after all, especially with an icy beer to wash it down.

Lindsey watched Weiner as she busied herself with her equipment. When she turned to look at him he asked if the ET worked the same as an LP record.

'More or less,' Weiner explained. 'They used different bases for them. Some were aluminum. This one is glass. That gave the best quality but it was fragile. There's a thin compound coating on the glass, and the sound was recorded in grooves just like an LP, only they started at the center and worked out instead of in.'

She gestured hypnotically and a dozen dials sprang alight. She turned and grinned at Lindsey and Rossellini. 'Wanda the Wizard would be proud of me.'

The jingle that Sister Mary Joseph had sung for Lindsey came from speakers now, accompanied by an organ. There were three voices, three young girls singing, and clearly they had listened to a lot of Andrews Sisters recordings.

We're red, we're gold, we're green,
We're too good to be seen . . .

'I'm reading that into my computer now,' Weiner said. 'It's being digitized, and once that's done we can make any number of copies. As long as we stay digital we're safe — no deterioration from generations.'

Lindsey looked at Gina Rossellini. 'You think that's her?'

Gina Rossellini cocked her head. 'It's hard to tell. Which one do you think? 'We're gold,' right? That would be Gloria Dorato.'

'You think that's Sister Mary Joseph?'

'Lindsey, she's fifty years older. She was a happy, excited girl. Now she's a tired, sick old woman.'

Lindsey opened his attaché case and pulled out his micro-DAT recorder. 'Here she is.'

Gwen Weiner raised her head, a slice of pizza in one hand and a can of beer in the other. 'Here who is?'

'Sister Mary Joseph. She claims she's Gloria Dorato. Golden Glory.'

'That's a DAT machine? Digital audio tape?'

'Latest International Surety issue. Desmond Richelieu loves new toys.'

'If you have her voice on there — '

'Singing the *Glory Girls* song. Recorded yesterday.'

Gwen Weiner offered them a Cheshire cat grin. She took a bite of pizza, followed it with a swig from her sweating beer-can, and set down the can and the rest of the slice.

'Voiceprints are like fingerprints. A lot of them are a lot alike but no two are identical. And they don't change. Voices get deeper or stronger or thinner or drier or — anything can happen in a lifetime. But the voiceprint is yours forever.'

She extended her long fingers toward Lindsey and he opened the recorder and handed her the tape. She made a computer file of the jingle off the ET, another from the DAT. She turned off the speakers and let four wavery lines work their jagged way across an oversized monitor screen.

'There they are,' Weiner said. 'There's the line for red, there's the line for green, there's the line for gold . . . and there's the line for your Sister Mary Joseph. No question about it. Your sick old lady is Golden Glory. You can take it to the bank.'

'And I think I know what the fiduciary material was,' Lindsey said. 'It's the *Glory Girls* property. It's the scripts and the disks.'

'There were some *Glory Girls* comics,'

Gwen Weiner added. 'And a low-budget movie. I can check it out with the hobbyists. They cross over, a lot of them. They collect radio, they'll know comics and film, too.'

'What do you think it's worth?' Gina Rossellini, always practical.

Lindsey looked at Weiner. 'The scripts, probably five hundred to a thousand apiece, from collectors. The ET's, once I'm finished with them, easily double that. We'll hold an on-line auction. But it's the rights to the shows — the market for classic radio is just starting to take off. In a few years, those shows will be worth a fortune.'

Rossellini said, 'Just hold on. A radio show, comic books, a movie. Where did the money go? Where did the royalties go?'

Gwen Weiner said, 'WING. I'll bet my *tuchus*, WING held out on those kids. And the money wound up at FEN. I'll bet Falcon-Eagle owes Gloria Dorato a pot full of bucks. And won't they scream when she threatens to blow the whistle to the FCC!'

She turned and watched the sounds

tracing on the screen. 'We'll have to fight Milton Jeckler and WLDY and the whole Falcon-Eagle Network, though. They can be tough and nasty, if you doubt that I'll show you my scars.'

Lindsey took a sip of cold beer. 'I think the sisters are going to win this one. I think they're going to raise enough money to buy the condo building they're living in and turn it back into a school.' Then he frowned. 'But there are only the two of them. And they're both old, and one of them is sick.'

Gina Rossellini took his hand in hers. 'Lindsey, don't lose your faith. God is on their side.'

'So's your Uncle Aldo.'

'Right. So's my Uncle Aldo.'

'And so is International Surety. Listen, Milton Jeckler may be tough and Falcon-Eagle may be mean, but they'll be up against me. And if they get past me they'll meet Desmond Richelieu.'

Gina Rossellini said, 'I don't think they want to meet Desmond Richelieu.'

8

Old Folks at Home

Marvia Plum

The squeal came in sideways. The reporting person called nine-one-one, Dispatch sent the paramedics, the 'medics reported the subject DOA under dubious circumstances, and the case got bucked to Homicide.

Enter Sergeant Plum.

Marvia was working swing shift, cruising Berkeley in a black-and-white, when she caught the call. She monitored the traffic, phoned in to McKinley Avenue and told the watch officer that she was responding to the scene.

She arrived a microsecond behind the patrol unit. She spotted the maroon and white Paramedic ambulance in the courtyard of Autumn House, the converted Victorian mansion on North Jordan Boulevard that now served as a retirement

266

home for three dozen still-ambulatory seniors.

She tipped her hand to Jeff Felton, pleased to see one of the department's sharpest and most experienced patrol officers, and wondered for the hundredth time why Felton had never put in for sergeant. He could have had the promotion in a walk, she was certain.

The Victorian had been retrofitted with automatic doors; they hissed open for Marvia and Felton. The lobby was filled with heavy, dark, old-fashioned furniture. The walls were covered with red flocked wallpaper that could as well have served in a turn-of-the-century bordello as in the home of a onetime president of the University of California.

Old people shuffled through the lobby — once the vestibule of the Victorian — like ghosts. They stopped and stared at Marvia, residents of another world peering back to hers and viewing her dimly through the gray fog of time, then tottered away to their separate destinations.

A buxom red-haired woman in a

tight-fitting white uniform crossed the lobby to meet them. At first she appeared very young, then Marvia realized that she was closer to fifty than forty; the deception was the product of contrast with the old folks.

'I'm Anise MacDougald.' She held out a pale hand. Marvia took it, introduced herself, asked Ms. MacDougald if she was in charge of the home. 'I'm the manager.'

The doors opened behind Marvia. She turned her head and saw the crime scene technicians coming through. The coroner's bureau would be the last to arrive, she knew. Their work required the least urgency. The chief crime scene tech nodded to Marvia, then stood a few feet away, awaiting instructions.

More gray-haired ghosts, their skins transparent and their thin bones visible — or was that Marvia's imagination at play? — gathered around them, drawn by the uniforms, the youth, the living warmth of the newcomers.

'You'd better show us what happened,' Marvia told MacDougald. 'The paramedics are still there, right?'

MacDougald nodded. 'Upstairs.' She led Marvia and Felton to a linoleum-floored elevator. Marvia jerked her thumb at the evidence techs, summoning them to follow. In the elevator she asked MacDougald for a quick rundown on the incident.

'Mr. Collins pulled the panic cord. All our rooms have little panic cords, really bead chains. If somebody feels ill or falls down and can't get up, all he has to do is get to the nearest cord and pull it and we send somebody up to see what's wrong.'

Marvia nodded.

The elevator stopped and the doors slid open. As they stepped into the hall, MacDougald added, 'Mr. Collins pulled the cord. I ran upstairs myself. The old stairs are actually quicker than the elevator. He just pointed to Mr. Smithton. His roommate. We encourage our residents to double up. It keeps their charges down, you see. And the companionship is good for morale. Loneliness is such a problem for old people.'

The door was open and Marvia stepped inside ahead of MacDougald.

One of the paramedics had stayed beside the man lying on the floor. MacDougald nodded to the still form as if they were exchanging a friendly greeting. 'That's Mr. Smithton.'

Marvia turned back toward the doorway. She gestured Felton forward. 'You're in charge of the scene, Jeff.'

Felton moved forward and stretched a yellow crime-scene tape across the doorway. He knelt beside the body, looked up at the paramedic and started asking questions.

Marvia stood with MacDougald, observing. The body was that of a man in his eighties. It was clad in gray trousers, slip-on shoes and a long-sleeved plaid shirt. The hands looked like claws. The sparse hair was a dull yellowish-white except where blood stained it and ran — had run — onto the nondescript carpet.

At the sight of the blood Marvia knelt beside Jeff Felton and peered at the wound without touching Smithton. The surface wound was small but an ugly indentation in Smithton's skull indicated that it had been crushed by the impact. A heavy cut-glass ashtray lay a foot or so from Smithton's head, one corner splashed with blood. A pair of figures in silhouette had been etched into the glass, along with a few words, none of them in English or even in Latin script.

Almost involuntarily Marvia laid her fingers against Smithton's throat, searching for a pulse she knew she would not find. She stood up and came face-to-face with the paramedic.

The paramedic said, 'Only thing I touched was the body, Sarge. Soon as I saw he was dead and saw the blood I figured it was for Homicide, not for us.'

Marvia nodded. 'You did right.' She addressed MacDougald. 'You said his roommate pulled the cord.'

'Mr. Collins.'

'Where is he?'

'The nurse took him to the medical room. We have an RN on duty at all times. She saw there was nothing she could do for Mr. Smithton so she took Mr. Collins to the med room. He was very upset, I was worried about him and I asked her to take him to the med room. If he calms down we'll have to put him somewhere, I don't know where we'll put him, I'll have to figure something out.'

'Did he say what happened?'

'He just said that Mr. Smithton needed help.'

'I want to talk to him right now.'

MacDougald looked worried. 'I don't know. We'll ask the nurse. I think we may have to send him to the hospital.'

★   ★   ★

Hobart Lindsey

American Financial Resources and International Surety Incorporated had been business partners longer than Hobart Lindsey had been alive; their billions spoke with authority. It was a long-standing policy at International Surety, not put in writing in so many words but clearly understood: when AFR whistled the tune, I.S. danced a jig.

So the claim hit Lindsey's desk in a bright red folder that meant *immediate attention, top priority*. Lindsey opened it and read a few lines, then reached for the phone. Somebody had been running up bills on a stolen AFR emerald card. That was a common enough problem, all-out identity theft had become a widespread crime, but this stolen card belonged to AFR's regional VP. The card had no limit and the bills had piled up high and fast before the theft was noticed, and the VP was steaming.

AFR had a fraud policy with I.S. and AFR wanted its money. Lindsey's job was to soothe ruffled feathers at AFR, first, and to recover as much as he could of the loot — the merchandise purchased with the stolen card.

The card itself had been canceled, of course, as soon as the VP realized that it had been stolen, but that had taken fully 48 hours and the purchases were absolutely frightening by then.

Lindsey punched in the number for the regional AFR office and fought his way through the vice president's receptionist, her executive assistant, and her personal secretary. Finally he heard an angry growl and said, 'Ms. Whelan?'

'Speak!'

'This is Hobart Lindsey at International Surety. About your emerald card.'

'Of course about my emerald card. What are you doing about the fraud claim?'

'Ms. Whelan, that's an awful lot of money. It's an awful lot of money in any case, but retail purchases in 48 hours, it's almost as if the thief was trying to run up bills.'

'S.O.P., Lindsey, you ought to know that. Amateurs use stolen cards to buy things for their own use. Professionals buy fencible items. We're dealing with a consummate pro here.'

'Even so, Ms. Whelan. Two Mercedes, from two different dealers no less, and an Acura, jewelry, a Benny Buffano sculpture from a prestigious gallery, well, where else would you get one, half a dozen computers, top-of-the-line home electronics including a couple of flat-screen HDTV's, it's an impressive haul.'

'There's more than that.'

'I see there is.' Lindsey fingered the list in the folder. 'What did he buy from Patriot War Goods and Weapons?'

Whelan said, 'I have no idea, except it cost a bundle.'

'Ms. Whelan,' Lindsey continued, 'do you have any idea how the thief got your card? Have you made a police report? I don't see a copy of one in the case folder.'

'I made a report,' Whelan said. Her voice was raspy, as if she were an unreformed chain smoker or as if she'd been cheering at a football game for hours on end. 'If you want to know about it I suggest you hustle your little tail over to my office and I'll tell you what you need to know. I don't want copies floating around and I don't feel like describing this criminal's M.O. on the telephone.'

Lindsey agreed and reached for his jacket.

AFR's regional HQ was at 101 California Street. Ever since a disgruntled investor had showed up there with a personal arsenal and gunned down an office full of people before blowing himself to kingdom come, the guards in the building had been both more numerous and more diligent than ever before.

Lindsey felt like an astronaut when he climbed off the express elevator. The executive assistant he'd spoken to — his voice was unmistakable — shook his hand. 'Garrison,' he announced. 'Come with me.'

Garrison — Lindsey didn't know whether that was his first name or his last — had the dimpled chin and glittering eye of the MBA on the make. His suit couldn't have been more than three days old, straight from Wilkes-Bashford, and Lindsey knew that it would be discarded in favor of a newer model long before it showed the first sign of wear.

Executive assistant Garrison escorted Lindsey into Ms. Whelan's sublime presence and faded into the scenery.

Whelan's official digs resembled a plush hotel suite more than they did a business office. 'Jeannette Whelan,' the VP grunted. Lindsey responded with his name. She pointed to a chair and he sank into it obediently. Before he could say a word she said, 'I talked to your boss, Richelieu. He vouched for you. Good. What was your question again, Lindsey?'

Flustered, he opened his attaché case and pulled out the red manila folder. 'Uh, the total amount of this claim — '

He looked up and she locked eyes with him. It was like looking into the face of a great white shark.

'It's, ah, a great deal of money.' He dropped the folder; fortunately it landed back in the attaché case.

She nodded but didn't say anything.

'Ms. Whelan, you were going to tell me why it took you two days to report the loss of your card. And the circumstances of the loss.'

'Yes.'

'Well.' He blinked. Seen through a tall window behind Whelan, the sky over San Francisco was crystalline blue and the sun was brilliant. 'Ah, how did — ?'

'Brilliant racket. I wish whoever did it had come to me for a job instead. We can use that kind of brains in this business. Too many dullards and too many slackers today. Dullards. Slackers.'

Lindsey nodded. 'Yes. And — '

Whelan worked at a table, not a desk. The only break in the smooth surface was a plasmascreen computer monitor. She folded the monitor down into the desk, pushed her chair back and stood up. She removed her jacket and hung it on the back of her chair. She was wearing a white sleeveless blouse.

She raised her fists and flexed her arms, showing long, graceful muscles. 'What do you think, Lindsey?'

Lindsey blinked. 'Ah, ah, very impressive,' he stammered.

'Think I got these for Christmas?'

'No.'

'Hard work. Two hours at the gym every night. The rest of this organization heads for the corner saloon for their liquid tranquilizers but I head for Starwest Fitness Center and my favorite torture chamber. They think they have the good life but thirty years from now I'll dance on their graves, Lindsey, and then go out and run the Bay to Breakers.'

She pulled her jacket back on and slid into her chair.

'Very impressive,' Lindsey repeated. 'Very admirable. But about the credit card.'

'Right.' Whelan grinned in a manner that Lindsey was unable to fathom. 'Last Thursday I left work at the usual time and headed for Starwest. I went through my usual routine.'

'Please walk me through that.'

Whelan heaved a long-suffering sigh. 'Checked in, picked up a couple of towels, went down to the locker room and changed to my gym outfit.'

'Did you carry a gym bag with you?' Lindsey asked.

Whelan shook her head. 'I keep a couple of outfits at Starwest. They run everything through the laundry for me, it's part of their service.'

Lindsey jotted a note.

'Back up to cardiovascular for my warm-up on the stationary bike. Did a few miles on the bike, then to the weight room. Pumped iron for forty minutes, then back to the bike for a cool-off. Then some stretches and mat exercises. Then a steam bath, sauna, shower, and back to the locker room.'

'This takes two hours?' Lindsey asked.

'Just about.'

An amber light flashed beneath the tinted glass cover of Whelan's desk. She tapped her fingertip on the glass and the light went into a polychrome dance, then winked out.

Whelan said, 'That's when it got funny.' She did not laugh when she said *funny*, and Lindsey didn't think she meant *amused* at all.

'Couldn't open my padlock,' Whelan said.

'Combination or key?'

'Combination.'

'You sure you had the right numbers?'

Whelan's eyes widened. 'You must be joking. Of course I had the right numbers. It's a perfectly standard rotary padlock and it had always been perfectly reliable. I tried the combination multiple times, finally picked up the phone and summoned the manager. When I told her what had happened she asked the combination and I told her. Of course that meant I'd have to replace the lock, but that wasn't my concern at the moment.'

'No, of course not.'

Behind her, Lindsey could see into the windows of the office building across California Street. Someone was gazing down at the plaza below as if contemplating a swan dive. But in the sealed environment of these buildings that was no longer an option.

'Once she'd tried the combination herself a few times she conceded that I was right. She had to summon a handywoman with bolt-cutters to sever the U-ring. She couldn't figure out what had happened. Neither could I. I suspected that something odd was going on, so I checked all my valuables.'

'Including your AFR card?'

She looked offended that he even needed to ask that, but she replied, 'Of course.'

'And it was there?'

'In my card case. Everything looked normal.'

'But it wasn't.'

'Far from it.'

'All right. When did you first realize that something was definitely wrong, and how did you know?'

'Saturday night. Friday I went to the gym after work, picked up a new lock at the desk and had my workout. Saturday I slept in, as usual, spent the day with my succulents, and met a friend at the Iron Horse for dinner.'

Behind her, sunlight glinted off a huge jet coming in from the Pacific for a landing at SFO. Lindsey nodded and waited for her to resume.

'Melanie Price. She's my oldest friend. We grew up together in Belmont, went to prep school together, roomed together at Stanford. She's in line for city editor at the *Examiner* in another year. If the *Examiner* is still around. We meet for drinks and dinner once a week and we go to the Iron Horse at least once a month.'

This time the blinking light in her desktop was green. She tapped once and a message appeared in the glass. Lindsey couldn't read it upside down. Whelan scanned it, muttered, and tapped a reply on the glass. The desk went dark.

'Where was I?'

'The Iron Horse.'

'We never split a bill. We just take turns

picking it up. I gave the waiter my emerald card and he came back and said it was a canceled number. I couldn't figure that out. It wasn't as if I'd maxed out the card. Couldn't do that anyhow. My emerald is no-limit-no-question. One of the little perks of my job. The waiter said they'd gladly put it on a tab, heaven knows they know Mel and me at the Horse. But I said, never mind, I'll pay cash, and I did. Then I studied the card. It was my signature all right, or a damned good forgery. But it wasn't my number.'

Lindsey shook his head. 'I don't understand.'

'Neither did I. Until I put two and two together. Mel helped me. I used to be a systems analyst and Mel was on the crime beat at the *Ex* so we both know how to solve problems. We traced it back to Starwest. The way we figured it out, somebody got into my locker while I was upstairs. Maybe she had bolt-cutters of her own or maybe she was trained as a safecracker and just opened the lock. My God, a little pipsqueak combination lock wouldn't even slow down a professional.'

She raised one hand and looked at her wristwatch. It looked like a good one. Lindsey didn't doubt that.

'She must have timed it exquisitely,' Whelan went on. 'Either that, or just took one hell of a chance and got lucky. She took my lock off, took my emerald card out of my locker and substituted the phony. I don't know how she got my signature, unless she's some kind of instant copyist, or maybe had a miniature scanner and electronic pantograph.'

'How would that work?'

'I don't even know if such a gadget exists. But if it does, she could scan my signature off my emerald card and lay it back onto the phony card. Then she put it back in the locker and relocked the locker with an extra lock she brought with her. That would have bought her an extra hour by the time I got things sorted out with Starwest.'

'Why do you keep saying 'she?' How do you know it was a woman?'

'It was the women's locker room. Starwest is a coed gym but the locker rooms aren't coed. Even San Francisco isn't that liberated.'

Lindsey pondered. 'But why was the extra hour important? You didn't discover the theft until Saturday night.'

'The crook couldn't know that. For all she knew, the fake card scam — I think that was brilliant, by the way, I really admire it — might fail. And I'd cancel the card and send out an alert within minutes once I discovered what happened. Even as it is, I know that the money was spent within three hours. If the theft took place at six o'clock Thursday, those big-ticket purchases were made by nine o'clock that night. She must have had her program worked out to the minute. Not only did she get expensive goods, they're all fencible. I'll bet those cars are in Mexico already. Or in the hold of a ship headed for Japan. Or Kuwait.'

Lindsey frowned, concentrating. 'One other question.'

'Yes?' Whelan waited for him.

'The emerald card — your emerald card — has a no-question-no-limit feature. Did I understand you correctly about that?'

'Yes, you did.'

'Then why didn't the thief just grab a fortune in cash? She could use the card for cash advances, couldn't she? Why bother with these complicated transactions, buying cars and HDTV's and computers and fencing them for cash? Why not just take the money to start with?'

'I thought of that myself, Lindsey. And here's the answer. While the emerald card has no limit, the AFR card cash fund itself has a limit. Even American Financial Resources doesn't have an inexhaustible cornucopia of plenty. So AFR Central monitors the cash account balance in real time, through our computer network. If she'd tried to get too much cash, she would have alerted the system that something abnormal was going on, and somebody would have been called in to look into it. Maybe even me!' That brought a smirk to her lips.

'So whoever did this knows the inner workings of the AFR system,' Lindsey suggested.

'That's right. It might be an inside job. But whether it is or not — this is a smart broad we're dealing with.' She ground out the words like small, sharp rocks. 'But I'm a smarter broad. And I'm gonna burn her ass!'

★   ★   ★

Marvia Plum

Marvia Plum left Jeff Felton in charge of the crime scene and had Anise MacDougald take her to the Autumn House infirmary. MacDougald introduced her to the nurse, Amy Brown. The nurse had dark mocha skin and was overweight and friendly and was sitting beside Jack Collins, holding both his hands.

Marvia introduced herself, staring all the while at Collins. For an instant she thought she knew him, then realized that he seemed familiar because he looked so much like the dead Henry Smithton. Both men were short, probably shorter than they had been in earlier decades. Both had pale, almost transparent skin. Collins' hair was pure white while Smithton's had shown the remnants of

287

once being blond.

Even their eyes were a similar color, but Collins' eyes shone with life while Smithton's had held the glaze of death.

Collins was staring straight ahead, moving his lips silently and nodding from time to time. Marvia had no idea what he was saying. She stood in front of him and took his hands from Amy Brown. She introduced herself and asked Collins if he would speak with her.

He raised his eyes to hers, paused, then nodded.

'Mr. Collins, do you want to tell me what happened?'

'The Nazi is dead,' he whispered.

'The Nazi?'

'The Nazi is dead.'

'Mr. Collins, your roommate is dead. Henry Smithton is dead. It looks as if somebody hit him in the head with a heavy glass ashtray.'

Nurse Brown interrupted. 'We don't allow smoking here at Autumn House. Health and safety code, Miz, uh, Officer.'

'Did somebody do it to Mr. Smithton, Mr. Collins? Did someone hit him? Do you know who hit him? Or could it have been an accident?' Among younger men, it would surely not have been an accident. But among these frail, aged people, a loose shoelace, a ripple in the carpet, a momentary loss of balance, and you could have injury or death.

'I should have done it years ago,' Collins said. 'Years ago. The Nazi. But I was never certain. He could lie and lie.' He nodded in agreement with himself. Then he added, 'So could I.' He smiled a secretive, inward-turning smile.

Should she mirandize him? Should she take him into custody? *Could* she take him into custody? It certainly looked as if he had wielded the heavy glass weapon, but there was no way she could book him into City Jail. She'd have to take him to the county hospital and have him admitted to a locked facility — if she decided to take him into custody at all.

'Mr. Collins, can you tell me what happened today? What happened to Mr. Smithton?'

'He had a visitor. His daughter came to see him. She brought it.'

Marvia turned to Amy Brown, then to Anise MacDougald. She tensed, sending her question telepathically first to the nurse then to the facility manager.

MacDougald answered. 'I'll get the log.' She disappeared from the infirmary, returned almost at once with a notebook. She laid it in front of Marvia, then ran her finger down the page. 'Here it is. Marjorie Dowling. Mr. Smithton's daughter. She brought him here, she visits regularly.'

Marvia blinked. 'Don't you control access to this building? All these old people must be — vulnerable.'

'We do our best. We ask everyone to sign in and out. We keep a file of authorized visitors with each guest's records, and their photos. But this isn't a prison, you know, Sergeant. We operate more or less on the honor system. But you see — *Marjorie Dowling* — *in* — *out*. She was only upstairs for fifteen minutes.'

'What about the ashtray?'

Mr. Collins was tugging at Marvia's hands. 'The ashtray, the ashtray,' he whispered. 'It was the monsters. Both of the monsters. Both of them!'

'I don't understand, Mr. Collins. What monsters are those?' If the old man was delusional, seeing monsters in ashtrays, he might have thought that Smithton was one of them. He would have picked up the ashtray . . .

Could Collins have picked up the ashtray at all? Marvia wondered. The aged man with his pipestem arms, his thin, fragile bones and withered muscles? It was heavy glass, it must have weighed the better part of ten pounds.

But if he was panicked by his imagined monsters, he might have found the strength to lift the heavy glass implement and bring it down just once, its sharp corner colliding with Smithton's thin temple. Once would have been enough.

'Did you do it, Mr. Collins?'

She was getting close to Miranda territory, she knew that. But if Collins was willing to speak freely, to offer a spontaneous statement, she should be able to use it. But that would mean she was putting together a homicide case, which would mean that he couldn't have been delusional.

'I should have done it a long time ago.' He smiled up at her.

'Why is that, Mr. Collins?'

'You weren't there. You didn't see. He looked at the monsters and he — ' He stopped speaking and a series of expressions raced across his features, anger, terror, grief.

Through all their conversation, Marvia had been standing in front of Collins, holding his hands in her own. Now he dropped his face and wept, his tears falling on the backs of Marvia's hands.

He pulled himself erect and dropped her hands. Nurse Amy Brown handed him a wad of tissue paper and he blotted his eyes. He reached for Marvia's hands and blotted them as well. 'My apologies.' A gentleman.

'Mr. Collins.' She decided to try once again. 'Who were these monsters you saw? Where were they?'

'In the ashtray.'

'You mean — like in the ashes? Like seeing the devil in a flame?'

'No, no,' he shook his head. 'The devil, I'd take my dinner with the devil, I'd drink wine with the devil before these two. With the devil I'd play pinochle before these two.'

'Then I don't understand.'

'I won't even say their names. My mouth I won't soil by speaking those syllables. I could never spit enough to make my mouth clean if I said those names. At my age I don't have enough saliva.'

Marvia turned. 'Ms. MacDougald, can you call upstairs to Mr. Collins' room and get Officer Felton on the line for me? Thank you.'

A moment later MacDougald handed her the phone. She asked Felton to sign for the ashtray and bring it down to the infirmary in an evidence bag. The techs could safeguard the crime scene until the coroner's squad arrived to remove the body.

To Collins she said, 'Sir, I have to ask you, Do you understand what happened upstairs? Do you understand what's going on now, who I am?'

The old man smiled wistfully. 'You know the best thing about Alzheimer's,

Miss Police Sergeant? Those are sergeant's stripes, yes? At my age, your eyes aren't always so reliable. You know the best thing about Alzheimer's? You meet interesting new people every day.'

Marvia said nothing.

Collins said, 'Ah, I'm so old I can't even get a laugh no more. Well, a Henny Youngman I never was anyhow. So, Miss Police Sergeant, ask me again the question.'

'Do you understand what happened, sir? Do you understand where you are and who I am?'

'Oh, yes.' He nodded. 'Oh, yes, believe me I understand.'

'It looks as if Mr. Smithton was the victim of a homicide. If you're willing to chat with me about it, informally, we can chat. But if you want your Miranda rights, I'll read them to you and — '

The old man laughed. 'I know my rights. I watch TV. What else do I have to pass the time? I see cop shows galore, Miss Sergeant. I know the niceties from NY to LA and back. Don't worry your head about my rights.'

The door swung back and Jeff Felton entered. At Marvia's direction he carefully placed the ashtray, still in its bag, on a counter.

Marvia said, 'Mr. Collins, would you pick that up for me?'

Collins swung around and peered at the ashtray.

'You want me to pick that up?'

'Please.'

The old man rose unsteadily to his feet. Moving slowly, he crossed the short distance to the counter. He slid one hand under either end of the heavy ashtray. His powdery white face reddened with effort. The ashtray did not budge.

★ ★ ★

Hobart Lindsey

International Surety had opened a prestigious regional headquarters in the upper reaches of the Transamerica Pyramid. Lindsey walked there easily from 101 California, rose skyward in an express elevator and used his Special Projects Unit ID to borrow a private office.

He was concerned over the timeline in Jeannette Whelan's story. If, as she claimed, she had reached the Starwest gym at six o'clock on Thursday night, and if the thief had completed her illicit purchases by nine o'clock, that meant that she had bought three automobiles, something close to a truckload of computers and other office equipment, an expensive sculpture and two of the most advanced television sets in existence in less than three hours.

Didn't the stores ever close around this town?

A few telephone calls settled that problem. The purchases had been arranged in advance. The customer had arranged to come back, pay for everything, and take delivery between six and nine o'clock Thursday night.

'Well, actually,' a nervous Mercedes salesman told Lindsey, 'she was going to come in Tuesday night. She never showed up, but she postponed to Wednesday. She's a V-VIP, you know, and we try to accommodate. She's a vice president up at AFR and she got stuck in a meeting and she actually had her executive assistant call us. A very impressive person, very authoritative. What was his name, now? Garrison, yes. Bernard, no, Barnard Garrison. He was all apologies but I could tell that he didn't like apologizing. Still, he explained Ms. Whelan's situation and of course we said, well, certainly. I mean, when someone has committed to a purchase of this magnitude, one does everything to accommodate. But everything.'

Lindsey said, 'Wednesday.'

'That's right.'

'She bought the car Wednesday?'

'No, Ms. Whelan's assistant called again Wednesday night and apologized again in behalf of Ms. Whelan. He said she was positively humiliated, she'd like to buy our whole staff dinner at the Carnelian Room to make up for the inconvenience, and could she pick up the car on Thursday. And we acceded, of course. My manager was hovering like a vulture and of course we agreed to do what the customer requested, and Thursday night Ms. Whelan did arrive with her assistant. A very charming, delightful person, I might add. She paid on the spot and they took delivery and drove off.'

'Paid how?'

'AFR emerald card.'

'You didn't check to see if the card was legitimate?'

'But I did. I punched it into the system and it came up clean but just to be certain I called the AFR 800 number and spoke with a human being who told me this was one of their NLNQ's. I asked what that was and she said, and I quote on this, Mr. Lindsey, 'no limit, no questions.''

Lindsey thanked the salesman.

The salesman said, 'Were we scammed, sir?'

Lindsey thought for a while before he answered. Finally the salesman said, 'Sir? Are you there, sir?' And Lindsey said, 'No, you weren't scammed. You sold the car. Congratulations. But I don't think you'd better count on that dinner at the Carnelian Room.'

The story was the same with the second Mercedes dealer, with the Acura dealer, with a very-very upper-upper Post Street art gallery, three computer stores, two home-electronics stores, and the city's top-rated, cutting-edge, we-always-have-everything-first-and-you'll-pay-through-the-nose-if-you-want-it, television dealer.

There was no telephone listing for Patriot War Goods and Weapons, Incorporated, but there was an address in the blazing red case folder so Lindsey decided to visit the establishment in person. He picked up a cab in front of the Pyramid and gave the cabbie the address.

The cabbie was a grizzled veteran. His African features were covered with a week's worth of white bristles and a snowy fringe peeked out from beneath his old-fashioned cab driver's military-style cap. He craned his neck to get a good look at Lindsey. 'You sure of this, mister?'

Lindsey said he was sure.

'Sir, I gotta take you anywheres you want, just so as it's in the city limits. But I really don't think you wanna go to this address.'

Lindsey looked at his watch. It had been a long day and it looked as if it was nowhere near being over. 'Why don't I want to go there?'

'You're not from the city, are you?'

'Walnut Creek.'

'You do better in Hunter's Point, you look like me. You know what I mean?'

'Could I hire you to stand by, then, while I make this call? I wouldn't ask you to do anything improper. Just provide a little — '

'Local color?' The driver chuckled.

They cut their deal and the driver pointed his cab toward the Embarcadero. He accelerated up a freeway on-ramp and headed for his destination.

Shortly, the cab pulled to the curb in front of a ramshackle frame house. A couple of ragged kids offered to watch the cab for a small fee and Lindsey nodded to the driver.

They had to pass a metal detector to get through the front door. Lindsey had to hand his electronic pocket organizer around the sensor. There was no sign on the building, nothing to identify it as Patriot War Goods and Weapons. He wondered if this was a crack house, but inside he found himself surrounded by an astonishing array of military collectibles as well as modern weaponry. The proprietor was an African American in a blue pinstriped suit, spotless white button-down shirt and maroon silk tie. He was standing behind a display case filled with glistening Samurai swords and World War II Japanese helmets. He set aside the slick journal he'd been studying and gave Lindsey a curious look.

'How did you get this address?'

Lindsey showed his International Surety credentials. 'I'm following up a case of credit card fraud.'

The black man shook his head. 'I run a straight business here. I don't even like to take credit cards. I tell 'em to take a cash advance and pay me in greenbacks. But once in a while I'll make an exception.'

'You made a large sale last Thursday evening, to a customer who paid with an American Financial Resources emerald card.'

The other shook his head. 'No.'

'Sir, we have records of the transaction. There's no point in denying it.'

'No point! Get out of my store, and take your slave there with you.' He started to come around the display case.

Lindsey held up his hands placatingly. 'You needn't get rough with me. You order me out of here, I'll go. But the police will be in here before you can blink your eyes, and you can expect a visit from the ATF and very likely the IRS. Or you can choose to talk to me. That's all I'm asking you to do, just talk to me.'

Blue Suit backed a step and reached toward the display case, his fingers inches from the ornate handle of a Samurai sword.

'No need, brother. You want us out, we gone.' It was Lindsey's cab driver. Suddenly he was standing between Lindsey and Blue Suit, and suddenly he was half a foot taller and thirty years younger than he'd been when they arrived.

Blue Suit dropped his hand and leaned on the counter.

The cabbie was a small old man again. Blue Suit said, 'What do you want?'

'Someone came in here last Thursday night and made a large purchase, and paid for it with an AFR emerald card. I've seen the charge slip. The card was stolen.'

'I checked with the company. The card was okay. They said it was a no-limit-no-question card. I never heard of such a thing before. If they try and stick me for it — '

'You won't be stuck,' Lindsey reassured Blue Suit. 'But I need you to describe the customer. And I need an itemized list of what the customer bought.'

'It was some white woman. Never saw her before.'

'Describe her.'

Blue Suit pondered. Then he said, 'The Whelan chick, sure. Light brown hair, real light, with streaks. She colors it, definitely. About fifty. Slim, maybe five-three, five-four. Wearing sweats and running shoes, but no gym hanger-on, if you know what I mean. She didn't look real happy, but she slapped down that card and signed the slip, that's all I wanted from her.'

The description didn't ring any bells with Lindsey. Blue Suit called the woman the Whelan chick but she did not sound at all like Jeannette Whelan.

'Was she alone?'

'Oh, no.' Blue Suit shook his head. 'She had her man with her.'

Something gave Lindsey a hunch. 'You didn't know her. Did you happen to recognize him?'

Blue Suit broke into a big grin. 'Recognize him? Listen, I know him. His name's Billy Tarplin. My customers' names are sacred secrets to me, but not Billy Tarplin. That chump is too weird. Dresses like a fashion plate. Puts me in the shade, and I try to look good at all times, it's part of the image, you understand? But Billy is just too far off the beaten track for my taste. He loves that Nazi stuff. Plenty of customers for that, but Tarplin pays top dollar for first shot at new lots.'

'Do you have his address?'

'This is strictly a cash and carry business, but Billy's such a good customer, I have to send his orders out by truck. Late at night, too — you wouldn't believe the things he buys. He must be planning a revolution with some of his weapons. Heavy machine guns, bazookas,

BAR's. That chump even bought a .57 millimeter reckless rifle. But, hey, he didn't get anything illegal from me, you understand what I'm saying?'

Lindsey agreed that he understood what Blue Suit was saying. 'I just need to track down this one purchase, the purchase made on the Whelan AFR emerald card.'

'Here, here's what they bought,' Blue Suit told Lindsey. He showed Lindsey a customer order sheet. A ceremonial SS dagger, uniform cap with death's-head insignia, an array of World War II era German medals.

'I don't like Nazis,' Blue Suit said. 'I don't like Nazi paraphernalia. Brings out some nasty types. But it comes in from time to time and there's always a market for it. If I lose Billy Tarplin I'll never miss him. These Nazi nuts get off on that sick stuff, and Billy's the sickest of the bunch.'

Lindsey was busy jotting information into his organizer. When he finished he handed the order sheet back to Blue Suit. 'You won't encounter any trouble from AFR,' he assured him. 'I just need the address where you ship Tarplin's orders.'

'You didn't get it from me,' Blue Suit said. He pulled open a file drawer, riffled through folders and pulled out a sheet of paper. Lindsey reached for it but Blue Suit pulled it back. 'No way!'

But he held it while Lindsey tapped the address into his organizer. It was in San Anselmo in Marin County. This case was neatly triangulating the bay. 'If you hear anything from Tarplin or, uh, Whelan, give me a call at once, please.' Lindsey laid an International Surety card on the counter. 'Or you could contact the police,' he added.

'Yeah, sure.' Blue Suit looked at the card without touching it.

'There will be a very large reward,' Lindsey added.

Blue Suit picked up the card and slipped it into his pocket.

Lindsey started for the door.

'Hey, hold it there.' Blue Suit brushed past him. 'I have to let you out.'

The cabbie stepped through the door-way ahead of Lindsey. As Lindsey moved forward, Blue Suit said, 'Oh, yeah, there was one more thing those two got. The man was mainly interested in the hard-core military goods but the woman asked me about this one other thing that came in with a batch of Nazi merchandise. I had it in the case and she was interested so I said she could take it. I don't know what the hell it was doing with those other things anyhow. I threw it in gratis, and that's really something, for me.'

Lindsey said, 'What was that?'

Blue Suit said, 'Some ugly old ashtray.'

*   *   *

Marvia Plum

'What do you think, Jeff?'

'I really don't think he could have done it. He didn't have the strength.'

'Even in a special moment? You know, the father who lifts a car off a child, that kind of thing?'

Felton shrugged. 'Anything is possible, Sarge. But I don't think so. No.'

Marvia studied Jack Collins. He was sitting quietly now, clutching one of Amy Brown's big competent hands with both of his small, fragile ones. 'I don't think so either,' Marvia said. 'But I think I'm going to request a hospital evaluation. What's your opinion, Ms. MacDougald?'

'Actually, I think it would be a good idea.'

'Does Mr. Collins have any family we can consult?'

The old man reddened and rose halfway from his seat, then sank down again. 'Stop talking about me as if I wasn't here! You got a question, ask me, Policer.'

Marvia leaned back. 'I'm sorry. You're right, sir. Would you agree to a hospital evaluation? Voluntarily, that is.'

Collins tilted his head thoughtfully. 'In America, I guess a hospital is a hospital, eh? Not a murder house. No, I don't mind. I got nothing to hide.'

'And do you have any family, sir?'

'Not in this world. In the world to come, they're all waiting for me. We got caught in the middle. In Poland. The ones Hitler didn't kill, Stalin killed. Our great friend and protector, Comrade Stalin.'

Now Marvia was confused. 'I'm sorry. Jack Collins? Is that a Polish name?'

'Jack Collins. So.' He shrugged. 'In

308

Poland, Jacob Chmelkovitz, in America, Jack Collins.'

'No children, grandchildren, no wife?'

'The monsters got them all. Why didn't they get me? I don't know, Policer, I don't know, I wish they had.'

Marvia said, 'Jeff, call this in, will you? Let's make sure Mr. Collins gets good treatment.' She turned back to Collins. 'They'll have an ambulance out here for you in a little while.'

Collins shrugged again, turning his hands palm up as if to show that they were empty. 'I could ride in your car, too, but I don't mind the ambulance neither.'

Once Jack Collins was taken care of, Marvia went to the Autumn House office with Anise MacDougald. She asked to see their records on both Collins and the victim, Henry Smithton.

MacDougald hesitated briefly, muttering something about confidentiality, but finally she acceded.

Collins' record was as he'd indicated. Born in Lodz, Poland, in 1914 as Jacob Chmelkovitz. One brother, three sisters. Married in 1932. Twin girls born 1935, no other children. Twins taken by Nazis for genetic experimentation in 1942, never heard of again. Parents died of starvation. Brother and sisters all killed in Warsaw ghetto uprising. Chmelkovitz imprisoned at Bergen-Belsen, liberated 1945. Classified as displaced person, admitted to US on humanitarian grounds in 1947. Changed name to Collins, worked for Post Office Department, 1948 to 1979. Retired.

There were no photos of authorized visitors in the file.

Smithton's was far less dramatic. Born Bayonne, New Jersey, 1916. Worked in war plant assembling trucks during World War II. Married, 1948; daughter Marjorie born same year. Wife deceased. Daughter married and widowed, name Marjorie Dowling. There was a photo of Marjorie in the file, and one of another authorized visitor, a man named Barnard Garrison. Marvia asked MacDougald for copies of the photos; MacDougald ran them through a copier and gave her one of each. Since Dowling was Smithton's next of kin and his designated emergency contact, her telephone number and address were included. She lived in San Anselmo, up in Marin County.

Apparently Marjorie Dowling cared for her father, at least enough to visit him at Autumn House. Marvia would contact her with the sad news. She would also have some very serious questions for Ms. Dowling about the heavy ashtray that had crushed Henry Smithton's skull.

★   ★   ★

Hobart Lindsey

'You a pretty standup guy for a overweight, middle-aged white man.'

Lindsey decided to take that as a compliment and thanked the cabbie for backing him up in his confrontation with Blue Suit.

'Thanks are nice, they don't buy no groceries.'

'You'll get a good piece of change for this day's work,' Lindsey told him. It was I.S. money, not his own. He could afford to be generous. And the cabbie had certainly earned it. The cab was untouched

311

when they reached it outside Patriot War Goods and Weapons, and the cabbie rather than Lindsey had paid off the kids who had guarded it so well.

The cabbie dropped Lindsey at the Civic Center station of the commuter rail line. Lindsey paid him off, reimbursed him for his time and the out-of-pocket expense that had gone to the kids, and added a very generous tip.

'Any time you need my help, cap,' the cabbie offered. He pulled a stub of a pencil out of his pocket, found a soiled envelope and wrote his name and telephone number. He handed them over. Lindsey thanked him and climbed from the cab.

The train would carry him to Walnut Creek along with hundreds of other commuters, shoppers, and students returning from a long day at San Francisco State or USF.

The train barreled through the tube beneath San Francisco Bay, roared above ground in West Oakland, ducked into another dark tunnel downtown, then emerged for its run to the East Bay suburbs. Lindsey sat with his pocket organizer in his hands, reviewing the case.

Somebody inside AFR understood the card system well enough to know that no-limit-no-questions wasn't as simple as it sounded. A scam artist with a stolen no-no emerald card looking for the main chance would have to buy and fence big-ticket merchandise rather than go for a killing in cash. How many people in AFR were thoroughly familiar the system? There must be dozens, maybe hundreds, starting with Jeannette Whelan herself.

And somebody at Starwest, a woman, had to know Whelan's routine and be able to get in and out of the locker room fast, without being detected. Whoever was doing this had set up her caper for Tuesday, then had to postpone it to Wednesday and finally to Thursday before it worked. She was smart, quick, and self-controlled enough to put off her action twice, waiting for the right moment.

He didn't know who the woman, the false Jeannette Whelan, was, or where she was. But he had an address for Billy Tarplin.

He climbed into his car and started for San Anselmo.

It was a long drive from Lindsey's home to the Richmond Bridge, through downtown San Rafael and past one Marin County bedroom community after another before reaching San Anselmo.

Billy Tarplin lived in a modest single-story home on a curving road. The neighborhood had the look and feel of a 1950s development. The original home-owners would all have sold their houses and moved away by now, or died off and left them to their adult children.

Ten-year-old cars lined the street. There was a tangible feeling of seediness and slow deterioration in the air. Most of the houses had small swimming pools. Children shrieked under the watchful eyes of overweight mothers smoking cigarettes.

Lindsey double-checked the house number, then rang the doorbell. He heard muffled sounds, as if someone was stumbling around inside the house, sobs and fragments of speech.

He tried the door and it swung open.

A woman handed him something and

he took it instinctively. It was sticky. It was covered with blood. It was a ceremonial dagger decorated with a swastika and Nazi eagle.

The woman was sobbing and babbling. She was spattered with blood, blood in her blonde-streaked light brown hair, blood on her white tee shirt and khaki shorts, blood on her face, her bare arms and legs and running shoes.

Lindsey heard a car screech to a stop and a voice behind him call out, 'Freeze!'

He turned toward the voice. The blood-covered woman was behind him now. He was holding the bloody dagger. A black and white police cruiser stood in the driveway and a uniformed police officer was pointing her service automatic at him.

'Bart?' There was shock in her voice.

'Marvia.'

'Put the weapon on the ground.'

He obeyed.

'What's going on here?'

'I don't know. I just got here. I opened the door and she handed me the knife.'

Marvia Plum moved past Lindsey. She

addressed the blood-soaked woman. 'Are you all right? What happened?'

'It's all over now,' the woman said. 'All over. The Nazis are dead. Both dead.'

Marvia asked, 'Are you wounded?'

'No.' The woman shook her head. She seemed calm now, and fairly coherent although dazed. 'I — he's in the pool. Come on, I'll show you.'

Marvia said, 'Come along, Lindsey. Stay where I can see you.'

The three of them walked through the house, out the back door into a modest, fenced yard. The pool was filled and the water was stained with a pink cloud. A fully clothed man was floating face down in the pool.

Marvia holstered her weapon and picked up a long-handled leaf net. She used it to draw the man to the edge of the pool. 'Come on, help me.'

With Lindsey's assistance she dragged the man from the water and turned him onto his back on the concrete apron. She felt for a pulse but there was never any chance that she would find one. There were major wounds in the chest and abdomen, and one in the throat that would have been fatal even if the others had not been.

'He was right,' the blood-covered woman said. 'I wouldn't believe him but he was right. So now — so now — so now it's all over, it's all right, it's all over.'

Marvia led the woman to a chair. She directed Lindsey to another. Lindsey watched, half in a state of shock, and listened as she asked the woman her name.

'Mrs. Dowling. Marjorie Dowling. Marjorie Smithton Dowling. Marjorie von Schmitt.'

Marvia shook her head. 'What's that? I don't understand.'

'I killed Billy,' the blood-stained woman said. 'I killed my daddy and I killed my boyfriend. Bill Tarplin is dead dead dead.' She grinned crazily.

'That's Bill Tarplin?' Marvia asked.

'Yes.'

Lindsey shook his head. 'That's Garrison. That has to be Barnard Garrison.' Marvia Plum shot him a sharply questioning glance. 'I met him at Jeannette Whelan's office. He was her executive assistant.'

'Who the hell is Jeannette Whelan?' Marvia asked.

'She's a VP at American Financial Resources. She was the victim of a credit card scam. If that's Billy, what's his name, Tarplin, he worked for AFR under the name of Barnard Garrison. He was the inside man on the scam. Mrs. Dowling here, I take it, was the outsider. Garrison got the information inside AFR. Mrs. Dowling stole a no-limit emerald credit card from Ms. Whelan's locker at the Starwest Spa in San Francisco. They cleaned up on it. Cars, HDTV's — and Nazi paraphernalia.'

For the first time he looked around the house, as much of it as he could see through the back door. The living room was straight out of an Eisenhower era *Saturday Evening Post*, only the colors were faded and worn by decades of sunlight and use.

'Would you like to see my lovely home?' Marjorie Dowling asked.

Lindsey shot an inquiring look at Marvia Plum. She nodded almost imperceptibly and he said, 'Oh, I'd love it.'

Marjorie Dowling rose and led Lindsey on a tour of the house. He could sense Marvia Plum following them, observing them, mostly observing Marjorie Dowling. The construction and furnishings were conventional, almost banal, until they came to one ordinary door with an unusually heavy lock on it. Unusual for a door inside a private home.

A sly smile on her blood-spattered face, Marjorie Dowling said, 'This was Billy's special room. He put in the lock himself. I wasn't allowed in here, even though this is my house. My own house. I used to call it Bluebeard's secret room. Billy got mad at me when I called it that.'

She extracted a key from her pocket. 'He didn't know I knew where he kept the key. I took it and I had a copy made and then I put Billy's key back. He never knew.'

She slipped the key into the heavy lock and turned it. She swung the door open and reached for a light-switch.

It was like museum lighting, and the room — larger than Lindsey had expected — looked like a room in a Nazi war museum. Flags, posters, military regalia. A fully articulated lifesize dummy in Wermacht winter uniform crouched behind a machine gun. A portrait of the Fuhrer hung in a place of honor.

Behind him, Lindsey heard Marvia Plum gasp. He felt light-headed.

'Billy was such a good customer at Patriotic. He always used to pay with his own money, he never let me go there with him until this time. You know what else he did with his money?'

She led them out of the display room, back to a modest bedroom. Through the bedroom was a private bath. A jar the size of an ordinary spaghetti sauce jar stood on the counter, a thin residue of white powder caked in the bottom.

'Up the nose,' Marjorie Dowling said. 'I tried to make him stop and you know what he said? 'Herman did it, even Adolf did it. I'll do it, too.' That's what he said. He made a good salary but it all went up his nose. Up his nose and to Patriotic for his, his *hobby* he called it. Just a little hobby. Just history. Didn't mean anything. He wasn't one but he was one, I

320

knew. And he said my daddy was one and I said he wasn't, and Daddy always said he wasn't, but Billy said he'd studied, he knew, he knew Daddy was one and one day I'd know it too.'

They had drifted back to the living room, like an ordinary suburban home-maker entertaining two guests, but Lindsey could see that Marvia's eyes were fixed on Marjorie Dowling while her hand hovered near her weapon. At least she'd holstered the automatic, but she could draw it again at any moment. He was surprised that she hadn't taken over the interrogation, but she seemed content to permit him to ask the questions and Marjorie Dowling to answer them.

'Your father,' Lindsey prompted.

' — and the ashtray,' Mrs. Dowling volunteered.

Lindsey was aware that Marvia became suddenly attentive.

'He saw the ashtray. Billy was the only one who knew what it was. He said all along that he recognized my daddy from old photos, that he wasn't really from New Jersey, that he wasn't really Henry

Smithton, he was really Heinrich von Schmitt. I always hated the Nazis, I knew what they did, and he said my daddy was a Nazi who came to America and hid out all these years under a false name. He was able to get a complete set of false records made. Somebody helped him, I don't know who. But I know that my name is false too.'

'But you stayed with him,' Lindsey said.

Marjorie Dowling shrugged. 'I didn't know.' She closed her eyes, then opened them again. 'I did know. I didn't know. I did know.' She grimaced. She looked like Joanne Woodward suffering in *Three Faces of Eve*. 'I never knew and I always knew.' She began to cry.

'Did Mr. Tarplin kill your father?' Lindsey asked

'No. Billy didn't kill Daddy. I killed Daddy. Billy said, 'We're going to buy this ashtray. Nobody knows what it is but I know what it is.' Billy studied his history, he studied all the time. He had a degree in history, you know. From the University of California. He could have been a

322

professor but he made more money at AFR.'

'You killed your father?' Lindsey asked. He was trying to read Marvia Plum's mind, trying to get Marjorie Dowling back on track.

'Billy said Stalin sent that ashtray to Hitler when they signed their treaty. Their pictures are etched in the glass, with the pledge of eternal friendship in German and Cyrillic. And Hitler didn't even smoke, wasn't that funny? When Daddy saw the ashtray he knew what it was. He was so shocked when I gave it to him. Then he said who he was. He didn't deny it any more.'

She looked at Lindsey, then at Marvia Plum, then at Lindsey again.

'I couldn't stand it,' she resumed. 'I couldn't live with that. I knew what the Nazis were, I knew what Billy was. I knew who Daddy's roommate was, too. I knew what they did to him. He couldn't fool me. None of them could fool me. I killed my father and I came home and Billy asked me what was the matter and I picked up his favorite dagger and I pricked him. And he bled. I pricked him and he bled. Daddy's room-mate saw the whole thing at Autumn House, he stood there watching and then I walked out and came home and Billy was here in his special room, in Bluebeard's special room, and I picked up his new toy, his new dagger from Patriotic War Goods and I killed him. He was so surprised, it was really funny.'

As Lindsey watched, Marvia Plum stood up and took the few strides to Marjorie Dowling's side. She held up a pair of handcuffs and Marjorie Dowling held up her hands, unresisting and cooperative. Marvia muttered a few words of magical incantation to Marjorie Dowling, then she picked up the telephone and dialed. Without being told, Lindsey knew she was calling the San Anselmo PD.

THE END

We do hope that you have enjoyed reading this large print book.

Did you know that all of our titles are available for purchase?

We publish a wide range of high quality large print books including:
Romances, Mysteries, Classics
General Fiction
Non Fiction and Westerns

Special interest titles available in large print are:
The Little Oxford Dictionary
Music Book, Song Book
Hymn Book, Service Book

Also available from us courtesy of Oxford University Press:
Young Readers' Dictionary
(large print edition)
Young Readers' Thesaurus
(large print edition)

For further information or a free brochure, please contact us at:
Ulverscroft Large Print Books Ltd.,
The Green, Bradgate Road, Anstey,
Leicester, LE7 7FU, England.
Tel: (00 44) **0116 236 4325**
Fax: (00 44) **0116 234 0205**

BACK TO THE LEGION

Gordon Landsborough

The Brotherhood of Tormented Men is comprised of individuals who were prisoners, tortured in the underground cells of secret police in a dozen Arab countries. On a mission, they have crossed continents to rendezvous in the middle of the Sahara. When a travel-stained group of ex-legionnaires comes upon them, that mission should spell death to the men of the Foreign Legion. But death comes to men who accept it, and these legionnaires are fighters who refuse to accept death . . .

ONLY THE RUTHLESS CAN PLAY

John Burke

In the city of London, the *Career Development Functions* rooms are situated on the tenth floor of International Synthetics. There, people undergo the 'Fifth Executive Course'. The participants expect a gruelling challenge — one in which men fight for power — knowing that the going will be tough. But they don't expect one of their members to die in gruesome circumstances. So, is this a test of their reactions — or the insane ambitions of one of their own number?

THE CLUE OF THE GREEN CANDLE

Gerald Verner

Living in the village of Long Dene, best-selling novelist Roger Tempest is assisted by his secretary, Isabel Warren. When he unexpectedly disappears, Private investigator Trevor Lowe is summoned. But eight days later, Tempest's body is found, dumped at a roadside. The police establish that it's murder and they suspect Richard, Tempest's impoverished brother and heir to his fortune. However, Lowe remains unconvinced — even when Richard escapes police custody and goes on the run. Then there is another murder . . .